one or two things I learned about love

OXOXOX

Dyan Sheldon

CANDLEWICK PRESS

Copyright © 2012 by Dyan Sheldon

First U.S. edition 2013

Library of Congress Catalog Card Number 2012950623
ISBN 978-0-7636-6665-1

13 14 15 16 17 18 BVG 10 9 8 7 6 5 4 3 2 1

Printed in Berryville, VA, U.S.A.

This book was typeset in Berkeley Oldstyle.

Candlewick Press
99 Dover Street
Somerville, Massachusetts 02144

visit us at www.candlewick.com

one
or two
things
I learned
about
Love
OXOXOX

For B. T. D.

FRIDAY

All year you look forward to the summer, and when it finally comes, what happens? Not much. There's no school, and it's so hot already you sweat standing still, but that's about it. Nothing special. Life goes on like normal here at Casa D'Angelo. This morning, the human alarm that is my little sister—shrieking as if she was being yanked through the roof by a giant pterosaur—went off at approximately 6:31. (If my bedroom wasn't right off the kitchen, I'd avoid this, but if I didn't sleep in the old pantry, I'd have to share with her. Which is worse. I'd rather sleep in a tree.) Anyway, 6:31 was an improvement on yesterday. Yesterday, Zelda woke me up at 6:17 because the cat was on her chair. Today, it wasn't anything that exciting. She was having a meltdown because a cornflake missed her bowl and landed on the table. (NIGHTMARE ON LEBANON ROAD! Everybody head for the hills!) So then she got mad because I laughed at her. My mother pretended to bang her head on the fridge. (I *think* she was pretending. Sometimes it's hard to tell.) A start like that and you have a pretty good idea what the rest of the day's going to be like. If I didn't have to go to work and lived in a house with air-conditioning, I would've gone back to bed.

The farm stand doesn't have AC either, naturally, but the traffic creates a breeze. We had the usual beach trade, but otherwise it was a quiet day. Which gave me and Ely a chance to practice our juggling without the risk of hitting someone. The major drama was when the big black cat that lives up the road caught another seagull. There were so many feathers it looked like it was snowing. And there was enough shrieking for a horror movie (most of it mine). This is the third one that cat's caught so far and we're still in June. Ely's calling the cat Monsanto.

The lanes have AC, of course, so the whole Lebanon Road Mob went bowling tonight—Nomi, Jax, Sara, Kruger, Cristina, Maggie, and Grady, the guy Maggie's been seeing the last few weeks. Even Louie, since Mr. Kitosky's fishing in Canada. Normally, of course, Louie's banned because he videoed Mr. Kitosky pushing Mr. Ledbetter down the lane and into the pins at last year's tournament and put it on YouTube. (I've never seen anybody turn that shade of red before. It was truly awe-inspiring! I thought Mr. K was going to have a heart attack.) Louie says that it isn't unusual to have to suffer for your art. Mr. Kitosky said if he ever catches Louie with a camera in his hands again, he'll teach him what suffering really is.

Back home to sweat and reacquaint myself with hysteria. My family can make a blood-and-tears tragedy out of losing a key. Tonight's big drama was because when Gus's date came to pick her up, Dad called him Elroy. As in, "Hi, there, Elroy. Nice to see you again." Elroy was last week. This one's named Zak. Gus laughed at the time, but she went ballistic when she came home. She said sometimes she thinks Dad embarrasses her on purpose. (He doesn't.) Dad said it's not his fault that Gus is a serial dater, and if she wants him to remember the names of all the boys she goes out with, she should either make them wear name tags or date boys who don't look so much like each other. She said maybe she should start dating girls. (It wouldn't make any difference. He still wouldn't be able to tell them apart.) I said to Dad it must be a great relief to him that his middle daughter only ever had two and a half dates in her whole life. He said when were they? I can't blame him for forgetting. They weren't exactly worth remembering. (Only I probably will, because it's starting to look like they're the only dates I'll ever have.)

I was hoping something wonderful would happen this summer. Now I just hope I don't melt.

SATURDAY

This morning the screaming that woke me up was Gus, not Zelda. Gus couldn't find her new sandals. Obviously, I must have taken them to bed with me. Other people take the stuffed rabbit they had when they were little. I take my sister's shoes. I told her to get real and leave me alone. She wouldn't budge. (If there's one way my sisters are alike, it's that they're both as stubborn as bloodstains.) Gus said she'd looked EVERYWHERE. She couldn't go to work until she found them. I suggested (reasonably) that she wear something else. It's not like she has only one pair of shoes. (She could open a store.

No, she could open a chain.) Gus said she didn't want to wear something else. Of course. If you ask me, it's not just Zelda who has issues. Gus is clinically irrational. She wouldn't stop screaming. "I mean it, Hildy! You'd better give me back my shoes!" When she tries, Gus can yell loud enough to be heard in Alaska. I pictured all these Alaskans looking puzzled and trying to figure out who Hildy was. That made me laugh. Which made her even madder. The sandals were under the porch swing. Mom found them. I'm glad I'm staying at Nomi's tonight. Mr. and Mrs. Slevka went to some big antiques fair to sell old jars and won't be back till tomorrow. Nomi may be well known for her feistiness and her big mouth (my gran says that not only would Nomi argue with the devil himself, she'd win), but she's terrified of being home alone. Even with the new alarm Mr. Slevka put in. Which is fine with me. The Slevkas don't have AC either (because Nomi's father has principles about air-conditioning, not because he's cheap), but next to Casa D'Angelo, it's like going from a war zone to a twenty-star holiday resort.

Went to my pottery class this morning, but it was too hot for our usual Saturday tennis match. We all agreed we'd rather walk to Canada on stilts. So Nomi and I decided to go into town. The stores are all air-conditioned, of course.

Mom said, "Why don't you take Zelda with you?" (She has to ask?) Zelda wanted to know if we were going to talk about boys all afternoon. I said no, we were going to be discussing the international monetary crisis. She threw a purple plastic astrodon at me and put on her sandals.

The gift store's selling fans! Not the kind you plug in. The old-fashioned kind you flap back and forth in front of your face. Mrs. Gorrie bought a case when the first *Zorro* movie came out. She thought the movie would start a trend. Only it didn't. It's not exactly like having AC or even an electric fan, but you can carry it around with you and at least it moves the air around. So psychologically it makes you feel better. Mrs. Gorrie says it just proves there really is a good side to everything, even global warming, because now the fans are selling faster than water in a drought. Nomi and I both got one. I would've bought one for Zelda, but she tried mine and right away hit herself in the eye with it, so I didn't bother.

Went to Maggie's tonight for a barbecue. Her mother says it's too hot to cook in the house. (Maggie says Mrs. Pryce is afraid the heat's going to make the microwave explode.) Sara and Kruger had a band rehearsal, so it was the rest of the Mob, including Grady. Mr. Pryce was in charge, as usual, even though he always manages to set something on fire (besides the food). It's mostly an oven glove or a deck chair or the grass—some ordinary thing you find around your average backyard. But this time he set himself on fire. He was flipping chicken and his LICENSED TO GRILL apron suddenly went up in flames. Grady said that you'd think they'd at least make them flame-retardant, wouldn't you? Mr. Pryce was saved from a fate worse than death only by quick thinking from me and Jax. We threw the dog's wading pool on him. Louie, of course, filmed the whole thing. Mr. Pryce said he hoped Louie wasn't going to make one of his funny videos out of it, hahaha- ha. Louie said, "Mr. Pryce, would I put you on YouTube soaking wet, covered in dog hair, and holding a chicken wing in the air?" Mr. Pryce thought that meant "No."

Nomi and I had our new fans with us. Jax said that if they didn't do much to cool us off, at least you could swat flies with them. Entertained everybody for approxi- mately fifty-nine seconds by juggling lemons. One of them landed in Mr. Pryce's drink. He said it might be a while before any circus calls me. Louie said I might con- sider a career as a bombardier.

*   *   *

The new alarm was going off when we got back to Nomi's. Mr. Janofski next door was sitting on his front porch in his bathrobe and pajamas, looking like he was having a really long, sleepless night. (Mr. J's a big man who probably would've been a bull if he wasn't a human, but his pajamas are pink!) We started running to the house as soon as we saw him. Nomi unlocked the door and turned off the alarm. Mr. Janofski said next time it happens he's breaking in and ripping it out with his bare hands. Nomi thinks he means it. He used to be in the Marines.

SUNDAY

Woken up by the alarm. And Mr. Janofski roaring, "That does it!" Nomi figures the vibration of the newspaper hitting the porch must've set it off. She leaped out of bed like a gazelle being chased by a lion and turned it off before Mr. Janofski got out of his front door. Left it off and escaped to the tranquility and calm that is Sunia Kreple's yoga class, even though Sunia doesn't have so much as a fan in the new studio because she says the sound would break the transcendental flow of energy (and AC would shatter it completely). But like Nomi said, it's always hot in India, where they've been doing yoga for hundreds of years, and it hasn't killed them, so what the heck. Watched sweat drip off me in Downward Dog, but at least it was tranquil.

On the way home, Nomi and I went over to Gran's, since we were nearby. Everybody jokes about old ladies needing help to open the ketchup and change a lightbulb, but my gran's not that kind of old lady. She's the kind who wants you to help her put up shelves or paint the living room. She can open her own ketchup. She'd just finished fixing that wonky step by the back door when we got there. Gran loved the fans. She wants one. She said it was about time we got something you don't have to plug in or charge. Gran hates cell phones and computers and all that stuff. She won't even have an answering machine. She doesn't want to be in touch with people 24/7. She likes alone time. She says imagine if Romeo and Juliet had had cell phones. No more tragic love story. Just, "Don't do it. I'm on my way."

The parents were arguing when I got home. Because the washing machine broke again. My mother wants to buy a new one. My father says he can fix the one we have. But the fight wasn't about that. The fight was about all the other things my father's going to fix. "You're still fixing Zelda's stroller and she's almost ten!" shouted my mother. "Exactly!" Dad shouted back. "She doesn't need it anymore!" Left them to it and went next door to help Louie edit his video of the barbecue before my mom remembered about the deck. Dad's been building that for almost as long as he's been fixing Zelda's stroller.

MONDAY

Dreamed I was sleeping in hell. I kept begging the devil to turn on the AC. I would have cried, but I'd used up all the water in my body on sweat. The devil wasn't moved by my pleas. (He sounded a lot like Gus when he laughed.) He said AC was bad for the environment. "If God wanted you to have air-conditioning, you'd have a unit attached to the top of your head," said the devil. (He sounded just like my dad.) Woke up to screaming and shouting. If I ever wake up and the house is quiet, I won't know where I am. Dragged my limp, wet body into the kitchen to see what was going on. My parents were having an argument about how to boil water. Got a glass of juice and went to sit on the patio. Texted Nomi to see if she wanted to go to the beach. Then Cristina called to see what we were doing. I said Nomi and I figured the only way we could avoid heatstroke was to spend the day in the supermarket or on the beach, so we were going to the beach because we couldn't wear our new swimsuits in the supermarket. Cristina said she'd come, too. I said she must be nuts. Not only does her house have AC, it has a real swimming pool. Cristina said it would be nuts *not* to come to the beach. Her sister and her friends have taken over the pool like foot fungus. She'd much rather hang out with Nomi and me. And who wouldn't? There's been no official policy statement, but the Mob avoids the Palacios' place if Lenora's around. I know Gus can be a bigger pain in the butt than being injected with a horse needle, but next to Lenora Palacio, she's God's Gift to Sisterhood. You have to try to imagine what that means. It's like saying Gus is a very small snowflake and Lenora is Alaska. But I still bet Cristina would've stayed in the chill cabinet that is Casa Palacio if her boyfriend wasn't two hundred miles away teaching six-year-olds how to toast marshmallows.

Zelda refused to go to camp today, so my mother made me take her with us to the beach. (In this family, Gus got the looks, Zelda got the personality disorder, and I got taken advantage of.) Zelda, naturally, decided to be invisible. Which meant she wore a white robe that reaches her feet (it used to be Gus's, but she disowned it after Louie videoed her climbing in the kitchen window in it) and the enormous sombrero with MEXICO across the front that Gran brought back from her cruise to Cancún. Which meant Zelda was about as invisible as a herd of elephants with bells and lights on. It was excruciating being seen with her. (Heads turned like windmills in a gale.) So, of course, the beach was really packed. (There are obviously a lot more people who don't have AC or pools than I thought.) A couple of people wanted to know what was up with the sombrero and the fans. They thought we were in some kind of ad or something. Nomi told them we were in the video for a new band called Keep Cool, and they started looking around for the film crew. We left Zelda on the blanket and went for a swim (she's afraid of water unless it's in a container). We figured she wasn't going anywhere, since the only thing she could see was her feet. When we got back to the blanket, she was gone. Her robe was in the sand like a puddle, and the sombrero was on top of it. Nomi said it was like when the wicked witch melts in *The Wizard of Oz*. Melting is the one thing I don't worry about with Zelda. Cristina was afraid someone had taken her. I'd like to see them try. Let's not forget the time she nearly got Mom arrested at the mall because she didn't want to leave and Mom had to drag her to the car, screaming like she was being murdered. And then she told the security guards that she'd never seen my mother before in her life. Anyway, we finally found her at the snack bar getting an ice pop. Jax's dad had given him the afternoon off, so he showed up with a cooler bag full of soda and a fresh outlook. He and Zelda built a sand space station while Nomi, Cristina, and I sat under the umbrella playing cards. Zelda let Jax wear the sombrero. With her in the white robe and Jax in the hat, it was like *Star Wars* meets *Viva Zapata*!

Tonight my father decided to work on the deck, but he couldn't find his level. My mother said it was wherever he'd left it last. Like everything else he can't find. He said it wasn't. He wanted to know how he's expected to finish the deck when she's constantly moving his tools. My mother said she's not the only person who lives in our house besides him. In case he hadn't noticed.

Went back to Louie's to work on the editing. Who would've guessed when Louie's dad gave him his old camera to fool around with when he was nine that it would become an obsession? Or that he'd be so good at it? Really. There are actually people all over the world who wait for his postings. Now his father says he's afraid to go for the paper in his pajamas in case he winds up in one of Louie's videos looking like an escaped patient. Mr. Masiado thinks he created a monster. He won't be the only one. Wait till Mr. Pryce finds out he's on YouTube.

TUESDAY

Work today. It was really busy, so there was no time for Ely to give me a juggling lesson. All my favorites came by. Broccoli Man. Blue Eye-Shadow Lady. Green Pickup Guy. The Countess. Farmer John thinks we're so busy because we're witnessing a cultural revolution. He says nowadays folks want their vegetables to come out of the earth, not out of plastic. Ely says that's not why we're busy. We're busy because we're on the beach road and folks don't want to drive all the way to the supermarket if they don't have to. Especially when they're sandy, damp, and smell like seaweed. All I know is that my fan got a lot of positive comments from the buyers of ground-grown vegetables. Except for Broccoli Man, who wouldn't get out of his car until I put it away. But all the more normal people said that it was both practical and elegant. The Countess said the ladies at court always had fans. Blue Eye-Shadow Lady said she'd always wanted a fan but she didn't know where to get one (so I told her). Even Green Pickup Guy said he thought it was very elegant. He said I made him think of the movie *Gone with the Wind*. Ely wanted to know which part: when they burn down Atlanta? He said he figured it'd be a lot more elegant if I was wearing a long, ruffled dress and a hibiscus in my hair. Not shorts, a LOBSTER LILLY'S T-shirt, and a baseball cap.

Did some more editing with Louie tonight. We're calling the new video *Flame Broiled* and the background music's the really old Burger King "Hold the pickles, hold the lettuce" jingle. When we got to the part where Jax and

I threw the wading pool over Mr. Pryce, I finally understood what people mean when they say "I thought I'd die laughing." We both nearly stopped breathing.

Maggie showed Grady some of Louie's videos. Grady already knew the one Louie made of his dogs Hitchcock and Scorsese arguing over who was going to sit in Mr. Masiado's chair (over 900,000 hits on YouTube). He's watched it five times, and he always laughs out loud. He thinks Louie's a genius. Louie's smart, but I'm not so sure about the genius part. He can't even defrost, let alone cook. When his parents went away for that weekend in May, he ate nothing but cereal for three days. And let's not forget that I'm the one who did Hitchcock's voice, totally ad lib (*and* helped with the editing).

When I got home, the kitchen looked like we'd been robbed. All the cabinets were open, and there was stuff all over the counters. Only it wasn't burglars. Mom was out, and Dad was looking for the iced-tea mix. Zelda was on the floor, wailing like she was being torn apart by tyrannosaurs (she wanted iced tea). Mrs. Claws was stuck in a bag of Cheez Doodles—all you could see of her was her butt and her tail, and when I dragged her out, she was all dusty and orange. Dad was standing in the middle of the wreckage, looking distraught. I didn't have the heart to tell him that Mom makes iced tea from scratch. Went to my room. Was talking to Nomi when the quiet of the night was shattered by hysterical laughter. My mother was home. I wonder if my parents ever had a romantic relationship. It seems unlikely. Which could explain why Gus has never found anyone she likes for more than a few weeks and I can't even get a date.

WEDNESDAY

For a joke, I went to work in the dress Gus bought when she was maid of honor at our cousin's wedding. It's pink and long and makes me think of birthday cakes and koi ponds (birthday cakes because it's pink and frilly, and koi ponds because that's what Gus pushed the best man into when he made a pass at her). Ely thought the dress was hilarious. I've never seen him laugh so much. Some people stopped just because they saw me bagging potatoes in my prom-queen dress and fluttering my fan and wanted to know what was going on. Ely says that we should have one day a week when we both dress up. We could have themes. He figures it'd be good for business. The Countess said I added a touch of class to the stand. (And I quote: "If the Czarina was forced to sell vegetables, she'd dress for the occasion.") Green Pickup Guy says he's going to call me Scarlett from now on.

After Gus left on her date tonight, I found my dad standing in the living room staring out the window like there was something out there besides the Masiados' house and the road. I said don't tell me that spaceship's back. He wanted to know if it was Zak or Elroy with Gus. I said it was Abe Zimmerman. He said, "Who?" I reminded him that she dated Abe for a while when she was in high school. He's the one who backed into the mailbox. My dad said, "He's got a new car." I said, "Fair's fair. We got a new mailbox."

THURSDAY

Nomi says if she wasn't going out with Jax, she thinks she'd be interested in Ely. I said, "Ely who?" She wanted to know how many Elys I know, exactly. I said do you mean Ely Weimer? From the farm? He's nearly seven feet tall and he plays the ukulele (it's a sight). Though he is an excellent juggler. She said she thought I liked him. I said I do like him. Ely's great. He brings laughter to the world of fruit and vegetables. Selling tomatoes wouldn't be the same without him. But I never think of him like *that*. You know, like he's a boy. Not one I might want to kiss or share a fork with or anything. Nomi said, "Well, I do." I was astounded. I thought she was so into Jax that she never looked at other boys. (Or if she did, they might as well be turnips.) Nomi went all Nomi, slapping her forehead and moaning. She said she didn't realize that because she's going out with Jax she was supposed to go around with a blindfold on and never think that any other boy was cute or nice. I said I thought that when you're into one guy, you can't even think about anybody else. Nomi said I have a lot to learn about relationships. Gee, I wonder why that is. She said, "No, really, Hildy. Sometimes I worry about you." (And I *don't*?) Nomi said it's as if I got everything I know about the boy-girl thing from songs and movies. I said well, I obviously didn't get it from real life, did I? Since I've never had a boyfriend. I wonder if I ever will. I think I'm under a curse. The Hildy D'Angelo Dating Curse.

Lebanon Road Movie Club Night. It was Louie's turn to pick. Thank God. If it's Louie's choice, it's something old and interesting. Jax and Kruger (and Max when he's here and not sitting around a campfire singing "Kumbaya") always pick war movies, horror movies, thrillers, or thrillers set during a war with an element of horror. I usually make cookies, but it's so hot, the thought of turning on the oven made me feel faint. Brought chips instead. Maggie brought Grady again. They held hands through the whole show. When they left, Grady thanked Mr. and Mrs. Masiado for their hospitality. Mrs. Masiado wanted to know if he has a sister for Louie.

FRIDAY

I've noticed quite a few women carrying fans! Really. Nomi says that means we're trendsetters. How awesome is that? Usually I don't even know there's a trend going on till it's just about over. Will being a trendsetter make me more attractive to boys, or less? I think it could make me more attractive to some boys—the cutting-edge, first-to-have-a-tattoo-or-a-piercing type—and less attractive to others—the regular kind my parents would approve of. But since I'm not attractive to anyone, I guess it doesn't really make any difference. Nonetheless, I do think Mrs. Gorrie should give us commission.

One of Lenora's friends threw the cat into the Palacios' pool to see if it could swim. (It could swim, but it wasn't happy about it.) Mrs. Palacio loves that cat. She always says it's the only member of the family who never gives her a hard time. (Which is true, from what I've seen.)

Anyway, eyewitnesses (Cristina and her cousin) say that when she heard the howls, Mrs. P came charging out of the house like cavalry charging out of a fort in an old Western. Only not on a horse, but on four-inch heels. She went straight into the pool too. Mrs. P and Dolittle were both so traumatized by this experience that Lenora and her friends are banned from the pool until further notice. So tonight we all went over there to hang out. I think Louie was hoping Mrs. Palacio and Dolittle would fall in again, because he brought his camera, but if he thought he was going to make a series of summer disasters, he was out of luck. Dolittle's not allowed anywhere near the pool without his new life jacket on. It's bright pink. He looks like a chunk of bubblegum with feet. Mrs. P admired our fans. She said they reminded her of Old Mexico. I said I'd tell Mrs. Gorrie. It'll make her year. Cristina insisted that we all act like we were having the best time, since swimming pools were invented so her sister would be jealous. So we laughed and shrieked and splashed around like we were advertising fun. Until Mr. Palacio (who has the personality of a dictator troll) came out huffing and puffing and told us to "simmer down" or none of us were going to be allowed near the pool until they hold the Winter Olympics on the Sahara. Turned out that Lenora wasn't even home. Of course.

SATURDAY

Zelda put all her dinosaurs in the washing machine this morning (that's 176, if you're counting). She flooded the kitchen. Mom asked her why she did that. Zelda said because they were dirty. And after everything was mopped up and Mom got all the dinosaurs out, there was one sodden, mutilated thing left at the bottom of the machine. That would be *my* fan. Zelda washed my Scarlett O'Hara fan. She said she washed it because it was dirty, too. I said it was not dirty. How could it be? I've only had it a few days. She said it was after it fell in the toilet. So this is my life: a teenage old maid who sleeps in the pantry and can't even call a paper fan her own. I know it could be a lot worse. But it could also be a lot better.

Louie's parents are going to be married forty years in August. I started working on a set of mugs for them today. I'm making them with lids because Mr. Masiado always complains that if he leaves his coffee for two minutes, it's full of dog hairs, and Mrs. Masiado always complains that by the time she gets to drink her coffee, it's cold. Forty years! It boggles the mind. You'd think they'd have run out of things to say to each other by now. Or that they'd get tired of looking at each other the way you get tired of having cornflakes for breakfast every day. But they haven't and they're not. They're, like, the poster couple for True Love (even if they look more like the poster couple for Elastic Waistbands). Mr. Masiado says Louie was an afterthought. As in, "After Loretta and I were happily married for twenty-three years, we thought that what we needed was Louie to drive us nuts." (This is the one drawback I can see to being an only child. All the responsibility for making your parents happy lands on YOU. Whereas I can make my parents happy by doing nothing. And it's no big deal if I disappoint them, because there are three of us, so they're used to it.) Louie's present to his folks is going to be a movie of them from their wedding day till now. (Which means there'll be twenty-three years of them smiling and seventeen of them looking like they're waiting for the boiler to blow up.) August is still a way off, but it's been in the preparation stages for months. (Just having their home movies digitized took longer than the life cycle of a tomato.) Louie's really well organized for someone who's so eccentric. Now he's moving on to the production stage. He's got a lot of new footage that he's been secretly taking since January that he's going to mix in with the other thirty-nine and a half years of recorded family history. So since Nomi was out with Jax, Maggie was out with Grady, Sara had band practice, and Cristina was waiting for Max to call, I went over tonight to help him work on it. It's going to be really, really good. It has everything: humor, passion, drama, pathos, dogs—and Mr. and Mrs. Masiado dressed up for a masquerade party as Marge and Homer Simpson. Maybe Louie *is* a genius.

I had this really good idea while Louie and I were watching a clip of Mr. and Mrs. Masiado learning to tango (she kept leading him into stationary objects and then he dropped her, but they both kept right on laughing). If by the time Louie and I are forty neither of us has found our soul mate, I think we should marry each other. There wouldn't be any sex or anything, just companionship and someone else to pay half the bills. It makes sense. We've known each other forever. We really, really like each other. We make each other laugh. We have a gazillion things in common. And there's no one I trust more. Not even the D'Angelos. Maybe I should say *especially not* the D'Angelos. Let's not forget the time we went camping and I went to the bathroom and when I came back they'd all locked themselves in the car because they saw a bear. (You notice how nobody's first instinct was to warn *me*!) But I know that if I was in danger, Louie would go to the wall for me, just like I would for him.

SUNDAY

Maybe I spoke too soon when I said this summer was going to be about as special as toast. Because—even though I can hardly believe it—I HAVE A DATE! That's right, ladies and gentlemen. I, Hildy D'Angelo, the girl most likely never to be kissed, have a date. A REAL DATE! Well, I almost have a date. I mean, I'm *going* to have a date. And not just, you know, SOMEDAY. As soon as he calls and asks me out officially. *Would you like to go to a movie, Hildy? And maybe afterward we could grab a burger or something.* . . . And I will act surprised and say, *Oh, that sounds great*—Good grief! I can't remember his name! How can I not remember his name? *Oh, thank you*—

whatever your name is — that sounds great. I can't wait! Anyway, I'm too excited to say more about it now. I have to call Nomi and find out what his name is. I just wanted to put it in writing. Not because I think I'm going to forget again. No worries there. But in case it winds up having historical significance. You know, so if we fall in love and get married and have sixteen children, I can say, *See? That's what I wrote the day we met!* How romantic is that?

STILL SUNDAY

Nomi says his name's Connor. Only we're not sure if that's his first name or his last name. Nomi said maybe it's both. Connor Connor. I said right, and he has a brother called Johnner. Nomi said, "You can never marry this guy, Hildy. Think about what you'd have to call your children. Donna and Bonner and maybe even Zonner. It'll sound like you have a family of reindeer." We couldn't stop laughing.

*　　*　　*

So here's what happened. Nomi, Maggie, Sara, Cristina, and I all went to the mall this afternoon to escape the heat. We were having an excellent time like we always do. If I have to go shopping with my family, it's about as much fun as shaving under your arms with a dull razor. And no matter how long it really takes, it feels like it's at least a day. (A very *long* day.) But when I'm with my friends, hours vanish like bubbles. Anyway, after we'd been in every store we like at least once, we stopped at our favorite coffee bar for a drink. Cristina had to go back to where she'd bought a skirt because she'd changed her mind about the color again, and Maggie lost an eyelash somewhere and had to do repairs, and Sara went with Maggie so she could check on the blister from her new shoes without grossing everybody out, so I went up to order while Nomi stayed with our stuff. The guy behind the counter was new. He smiled. I smiled. (I have a normal smile, but he's got a smile that makes you think you've never really seen anybody smile before. It made me feel like I was a glass of water and somebody dropped two Alka-Seltzers in me.) He said, "What can I get you?" I said, "Three iced lattes, an iced mint tea, and a lemonade." He said, "Coming right up." And then he winked, and my heart stopped for a couple of beats. While he was getting our drinks, he said it looked like we'd been doing a lot of shopping, and I said, "Well, you know, that's why we came to the mall—that and the air-conditioning." And he laughed. I guess because he laughed at my joke, I got really brave and said I'd never seen him at Café Olé! before. He said that was because he'd only just started. AND THEN he said, "I would've started sooner if I knew you came here." It was a good thing I wasn't holding our drinks when he said that, or they would've been all over the floor. And then he pointed to his shirt and I guess he said, "My name's Connor," and I said, "I'm Hildy." He wanted to know if I came to Café Olé! a lot. I said, "Not as often as you do." And he laughed again. When I got back to the table, Nomi was looking at me like I'd found hidden treasure and she was waiting for me to tell her where it is. I said, "What?" She started laughing. She said, "Excuse me, Hildegard, but were my big brown eyes deceiving me or did I see you *flirting*?" I said her big brown eyes were deceiving her. I mean, have we met? I don't even know how to flirt. In my family, Gus got all the flirting genes. Nomi said, "Well, he sure looked like *he* was flirting." I said he was just being friendly. You know, like servers are supposed to be. I mean, good grief, everybody knows that. So they get you to buy more, because you think they're so nice and pally. "Oh, right." Nomi did her slapping-her-forehead thing. "I guess it's true what they say about additives in our food. I must've been hallucinating all that smiling and head bobbing and I-think-you're-hot body language because I eat so much junk." And then she blew her straw wrapper at me. But all the while we were having our drinks, I kept kind of glancing over at him. Casually. Quickly. Like my eyes just happened to wander to him by accident. Maggie said, "That cute barista keeps looking over here." Nomi made this innocent-little-me face. "Ooh . . . I wonder who he could be looking at?" Cristina peered over the tops of her glasses, "Did I miss something?" Sara glanced from me to Nomi and back again and said, "What's going on?" I said they didn't miss anything, and nothing was going on. I thought I sounded pretty convincing. "Ignore Nomi. She's been eating too much processed food. She's delusional." Nomi rolled her eyes like she was in some Broadway play. (She can be so melodramatic sometimes. She really should be in my family instead of me.) "Look at me! I'm delusional!" She said this really loud. You know, so everyone out in the parking lot could hear her. Heads turned. It would've been OK with me if the floor had opened up under my chair right then and I'd fallen through. But there's never a trapdoor around when you really need one. I told them to stop laughing so much or he'd think we were talking about him. Maggie said, "We *are* talking about him."

Cristina pointed at me. "Look at you! Something *is* going on! You're blushing!" My face felt like I'd been sitting on the beach all day without any sunblock. I said I thought we should be going and pushed back my chair. "You're acting like schoolgirls." Sara said, "Um, duh, Hildy. Don't look now, but we *are* schoolgirls." I said not little ones, we aren't. Nomi said, "I don't think Mr. Coffee thinks you're a little girl." She was practically purring. They were all still laughing and teasing me as we started down the plaza. Then all of a sudden somebody called my name. "Hey! Hildy!" I turned around automatically. He was standing in the doorway of Café Olé!, waving. "Hildy! You forgot something." I figured I must've dropped something when I was paying. Or fleeing. I'm always doing that. Usually disgusting used Kleenex or old wrappers. I ignored the sniggers of my childish friends and went back. "What?" I asked. "What did I forget?" And he said: YOU FORGOT TO GIVE ME YOUR PHONE NUMBER! Just like that. It was the most romantic thing that's ever happened to me. Like I was in a movie. (But not one of Louie's!) I'm not an expert or anything — I've only had the two and a half dates that nobody remembers (and the half doesn't even count) — but usually when a boy wants to ask you out, he kind of shuffles around and then blurts out something awesomely sophisticated like, "You want to do something

Friday night?" I think it must be a sign of maturity that Connor could say something so clever.

MONDAY

No call. No message. I didn't really have anything planned for today, so I spent most of the morning and afternoon just hanging around, kind of waiting. It was like waiting to speak in front of the class. (Which to me is a lot like waiting for your turn to be hanged.) You have to pretend to be listening, but all you can really think about is when it's going to be your turn. The difference is that when I have to speak in front of the class—or be executed—I'm nervous and terrified, and today I was nervous and excited. I know I'm being ridiculous. Even *I* know that "I'll call you" doesn't mean a boy's going to call the minute he gets home. It's not a promise. (Nomi says that most of the time it's more like a threat.) But I still kept checking my phone every ten minutes. I even called myself from the landline to make sure it was working. (It was.)

Was relieved that I had something to do tonight. The whole Mob went to play beach volleyball and then for pizza. Cristina acted all surprised that I showed up. She said she thought I'd want to stay home and wait for Mr. Coffee to call. I explained that the whole point of a cell phone is that you take it with you so you don't have to spend half your life sitting by the telephone waiting for a call the way people used to. That's why they were invented. To liberate us. Maggie said yeah, but I wasn't going to hear my phone when I was charging through the sand to hit the ball, was I? Reminded her that I do have voice mail. He's allowed to leave a message. And besides, I said, he can always call back, can't he? Cristina said, "Dig you, Ms. Cucumber. You're getting the hang of this dating thing pretty fast." Maggie said she didn't see how he could call back if he'd never called in the first place. She thinks she's funny. Nomi said I shouldn't worry; it's only been one day. Worry after a week. I said I wasn't worried Connor wouldn't call. Why would he say he's going to call if he isn't? It's not like I *made* him say he'd call. It was his idea. If you have the idea to do something, why wouldn't you do it? Sara said well, yeah. That makes sense. But personal experience suggests that it doesn't mean that's how it works. Kruger, who can remember any melody after hearing it once, never remembers when he's supposed to call her. Or maybe Connor changed his mind. It's been known to happen. So that all made me feel way better. I was jittery today because I didn't know *when* Connor would call, not because I didn't think he would. But the girls got me so worried that I kind of lost concentration and collided with Kruger. He thinks I broke his nose. Thank God it wasn't his hand.

No messages. Morale losing altitude. Nomi said maybe Connor lost my number. I reminded her that he wrote it on his hand, so it's not like he was going to throw it out by accident or anything. She said that maybe he accidentally washed it off. They have all those signs in the bathroom: EMPLOYEES MUST WASH HANDS. She says she's sure people accidentally wash off numbers they wanted to keep all the time. More often than you'd think. Which means that I'll have to go back to Café Olé! as soon as I can. But what if Nomi's wrong and that isn't what happened? What if he just changed his mind? Like Sara said. Then I can never go back to Café Olé! Not even if every other coffee bar in the county shuts down. This stuff could really make you crazy. My dad was actually working on the deck when I got home, so I gave him a hand just to take my mind off my phone for a while. I hammered his finger.

TUESDAY

I decided to start acting like a sane person again. (And not hurt anyone else.) If he called, he called. And if he didn't, at least I know that some really cute guy was once interested in me, even if it was only for five minutes. I left my phone home today so I wouldn't feel it in my pocket whispering, *No call . . . no call . . . still no call . . . are you sure you gave him the right number . . . ?* like some evil genie. I told my mom it needed a charge and to call me on Ely's cell if she wanted me for anything. We were really busy on the stand, and Ely was in super-hilarious mode, and Broccoli Man came and wanted *exactly* nineteen ounces of onions, so that took a while, and Green Pickup Guy also showed up and wanted to know what happened to my fan, and I told him about Zelda and the dinosaurs and the flood, and he was very sympathetic (he has two brothers), so the day went a lot faster than yesterday did. But as soon as I got home, I checked to see if anybody had called. Of course, no messages. Doom loomed. I called myself from the landline. Phone working just dandy.

I was in the shower. Where else? I mean, if you've been waiting more than forty-eight hours for someone to call you, when else would he call? I didn't even bother turning off the water. I just jumped out, dripping. There was soap in my eyes and water everywhere, and I knocked the bowl of shells my mother keeps on the toilet tank on the floor reaching blindly for my phone. (Why do we have fish on our shower curtain and a bowl of shells on top of the tank? It's not an aquarium; it's a bathroom.) Heedless of the risk of electrocution by wet electronic device, I pounced on my phone like a cat on a mouse. I said, "Hi." He said, "Hildy?" I didn't say *Well, who were you expecting to answer?* like I would've if it was Louie or someone like that. I said, "Yes." He asked me what I was doing. I didn't say I was standing wet and naked in the bathroom with soap in my eyes. I said, "Nothing much." He said he just got back from work. He said it was frantically busy all day. I said I told you, it's the heat. It's driving everyone into anything that's air-conditioned. Have you seen the buses? People are just riding back and forth for hours. And I bet the supermarkets are packed tighter than battery cages. While he laughed, I rubbed my eyes with a towel. Blind, but now I see! He's a senior at Priestly-Hamilton (or will be when school starts); that's why I've never seen him before. Besides the fact that he's only just started working at the mall. (And because I don't go to games. He plays a lot of games with balls.) He had some pretty funny stories of stuff that had happened at Café Olé! since he's worked there. He said he used to think most people were mainly normal, but now he's not so sure. I said that's what working with the public does. You realize that most people are a little nuts. And some are a lot nuts. We were laughing so much that he didn't hear his mom yelling till she started banging on his bedroom door. He said he better go. I said I had to go too. (Which was true. The heat had dried me off, but I didn't have any clothes on and the water was still running.) I had one leg in my shorts when my phone rang again. It was Connor. He said he'd been so involved in talking to me that he'd forgotten to ask me out. (How cute is that?) I'm seeing him on Thursday. It's his day off. (I don't want to start out by making problems, so I didn't say anything, but it isn't my day off, of course. I figure I can probably swap with Mike for one of her days.) He says he has a great idea for what we can do. He doesn't want to go somewhere noisy or crowded. He wants to go somewhere where we can talk and get to know each other. I said, "What? Group therapy?" He said it's a surprise. Oh, goody.

I don't want to get carried away or anything (Nomi says it's not pride that goes before a fall, it's HOPE), but I am getting kind of excited about the BD (Big Date). I want to believe that (at long last) the Hildy D'Angelo Dating Curse has been lifted. And that I'm finally going to go out with someone like other girls do. You know, instead of another immense disaster/public humiliation/waste of time/all of the above.

PAST
DISASTROUS
DATES

1 Mick Littlejohn in ninth grade. We went to a movie. Mr. Littlejohn drove us there and back. Mr. Littlejohn and Mick talked about football the whole time we were in the car. The last thing Mick said when we got to the movies was something about being tied with minutes left to play. When we came out two hours later, Mick got into the car and started talking about how in the very last minute some guy made a fifty-yard pass and his team won 33–30. I'm not really into football (I'd rather watch a snail race at night in a fog), but that's the kind of thing you remember. At least you do if it's the only time you heard your date's voice all afternoon.

2 David Schlessel in tenth grade. (This is the half date that doesn't count.) Nomi, Sara, Cristina, Maggie, and I went to the Halloween dance together. Safety in numbers. (And so you don't have to stand there all by yourself like the last doll on the toy-store shelf on Christmas Eve.) We went as a '60s girl band (no instruments and we all dressed the same). David Schlessel asked me to dance. We had a couple of dances, and then I said I had to sit down because it's really hard to dance when you're dressed like a '60s backup singer. My feet were redefining the meaning of pain. We hadn't talked while we were dancing, but when I was about to limp away, he all of a sudden asked me if I wanted to go out with him. I don't know if I did or I didn't, but I said yes. Turned out, he didn't want to go out with me. He thought he was asking out Sara. He didn't realize I wasn't Sara until I showed up at the movie. He wanted to know where Sara was. I said I guessed she was probably at home. He asked if she was standing him up. I said, "Standing you up *where*?" He said, you know, breaking our date. I said I didn't know he had a date with Sara; I was under the impression that he had a date with me. He said he

really had to have his glasses checked. There was no point in wasting money on a movie, so we both went home after that. (That's why it's only half a date and it doesn't count.)

3 Daryl Jonas last spring. Daryl sat next to me in math. He's about as good at math as a skunk. He's also immensely accident-prone. It's practically a talent. Every week it was something else. A fractured wrist (pulling himself out of the pool). A sprained ankle (stepping off the sidewalk). A black eye (he really did slam right into a door). Daryl can't walk into a room without knocking into something or someone. (He said his mother fines him every time he breaks something now, and Mrs. Spurgeon in the cafeteria made him bring his lunch from home because he dropped his tray so many times that she refused to serve him anymore.) But Daryl's nice and funny, so I ignored all the times he knocked stuff off my desk or got himself caught in my bag, and when he asked me if I wanted to go bowling, I said yes. He broke my toe. I was lucky he didn't ask me to go white-water rafting.

Which makes this the first time I'm going out with someone I really and truly want to go out with. And who really wants to go out with me. Someone who's hugely attractive, super charming, and a good conversationalist.

And who could walk through a china shop without putting it out of business. Sara says I shouldn't get too excited. She says not to forget the Frog Factor. I said what do frogs have to do with the rainfall in Oklahoma? She said you have to kiss a lot of frogs before you find a prince. (She read that in a magazine while she was waiting for her mother to have her root canal.) But Cristina says there's no point starting out expecting the worst, because if you do, that's exactly what you'll get. However, Maggie says there's a difference between negativity and realism. She says you should hope for the best but be prepared for the worst. And Nomi says that even though Connor's cute and there's no evidence that he starts food fights or that his feet smell like cheese, he could still be a disappointment. That's just the way life is. I said that's true. Life is like that. On the other hand, he might not be a disappointment. He might be the exception that proves the rule (as Gran would say). Life is like that, too. Nomi said if she was me, she probably wouldn't hold her breath.

Mike's agreed to swap my Thursday for her Saturday. She said no sweat. My mother wasn't as gracious, because most of the time she needs me to help with Zelda on Saturdays, since there's no day camp. She kept saying, "You're not going to make a habit of this, are you, Hildy?"

I said, "What am I—an indentured servant?" Naturally, she ignored that. She said, "What about your pottery? You're missing that too." I said it's only one day. What difference is one day going to make?

WEDNESDAY

I had a really hard time focusing at work today. I kept giving people potatoes when they asked for tomatoes, and tomatoes when they asked for potatoes. I put zucchini in with the cucumbers. I went to put a basket of onions on the table, and I missed. Onions went rolling all over the parking area. Blue Eye-Shadow Lady pulled in at exactly that moment. (Murphy's Law strikes again.) She flattened about six before she finally came to a stop. Then she burst into tears. She thought she'd run over a prairie dog. Ely tried to tell her that we don't have prairie dogs in this state, but would she listen? No, she would not. (Turns out she mowed one down in Colorado once and it scarred her for life.) I was holding up a squashed onion and saying,

"Look! It's not a prairie dog—it's an edible bulb!" But she was crying too much to see it. By the time she calmed down, her face was all blue. I was so stressed out after that that I overcharged Green Pickup Guy. "Scarlett, dear." He held out his hand. "I thought I bought squash, not gold." I apologized. Profusely. Later, Ely wanted to know if I was having some trouble at home or something, because I was so distracted. He said he knows how crazy families can get. (Ely's father isn't allowed within forty miles of Redbank without being arrested. That's how crazy he got.) I said it was nothing like that. I said I was finding it hard to concentrate because of the heat. No wonder none of the major inventions of the industrial age came out of tropical countries. Everybody was collapsed under palm trees, fanning themselves with giant leaves. (Unless their little sisters washed them after they dropped them in the toilet.) Ely said, "Whatever, Hildy. But I'm here if you ever need somebody to talk to." I said I'd keep that in mind.

The main reason I was all vague and preoccupied is that I can't decide what to wear tomorrow. Which is why I couldn't very well tell Ely. He was thinking heartbreak and fear, and I was thinking the jungle print or the skinny jeans. If I had some clue what we're doing, I'd know how to dress. I don't want to look like I just threw on any old thing if his idea of getting to know each other is a candlelit dinner at a nice restaurant, but I don't want to be wearing a dress and good shoes if we're going clamming.

Gus won't let me borrow her super-best peach silk shirt for the BD, even though it'd be perfect, since silk is casual and elegant at the same time. I said that I don't know how she can live with herself, being so selfish. She said she just about manages. And anyway, you should never go for broke the first time you go out with a guy. You want to get better and better each time he sees you. I don't know how she ever came up with this, since except for Abe (who wrecked the mailbox) and Barry Lincoln (who lasted almost a whole summer), she rarely has more than two dates with the same person. I argued that if I don't look really great, there won't be a next time. Gus said, "You weren't wearing my peach shirt when he asked you out, were you?" Of course not. I was wearing those cotton pants I got for yoga with the geckos all over them and a D'ANGELO'S GARAGE T-shirt. "Right," said Gus. "So how high can his expectations be? You looked like a beach bum. You see, Hildy, it so doesn't matter what you wear. It's you he's interested in, not your clothes." This from the girl who once spent so long getting ready in the bathroom that the rest of us had to go over to the Masiados' to use their facilities.

*   *   *

Have had everything out of my closet and my dresser
TWICE tonight. The depressing truth is that all my
summer stuff makes me look like a beach bum. A beach
bum who never goes anywhere. (Well, the beach, but
you'd expect that.) Except my overalls. They don't make
me look like a beach bum. They make me look like a
farmer (which is OK, really, because they're supposed to.
I got them at the secondhand store to wear to work). I
don't have anything that says *hot* or *babe*. It's all *lukewarm*
and *buddy*. Nomi said she'd lend me *her* peach silk shirt,
only she doesn't have one. And even if she did, it would
fit me only in a dream. The last time Nomi and I were
even close to being the same size, we were twelve. And
then I kept growing, and she kind of stopped. So Nomi's
what everybody calls petite or doll-like, and I look like
I'd be a good basketball player. (But I'm not. I always
duck when someone throws the ball to me.)

THURSDAY

BIG DATE DAY

After a restless night dreaming that I met Connor wearing the bunny suit I had when I was eight, I called Nomi as soon as I got up and she came over to help me pick out an outfit and get ready. Nomi was great. (Of course. She isn't my best friend because nobody else applied for the job.) She dug out those white jeans I never wear because I'm afraid of bleeding in them, a plain, pale-colored top, and that woven scarf in about eight different shades of blue that Gran gave me for Christmas, which I never knew what to do with. It took hours to do my hair and everything. But when we were done, I looked pretty good. Nomi said I was *definitely* all-purpose — you know, like I could go to anything from a ball game to lunch with the governor. Unfortunately, Connor's family doesn't live near a stadium or near the gubernatorial mansion. Where they live is on the lake over by Crow's Cross. Connor's surprise was that he thought it'd be a great idea if we went canoeing. (So it wasn't either-or; it was either oar.) "You can't get more peaceful, private, and quiet than canoeing," said Connor. (*Only in death* was what I would've said if he'd been Louie or Ely.) But even though I hadn't exactly been planning on rowing across a fairly large body of water, I did think it was sweet and thoughtful of him to want to get to know me like that. Most guys would just take you to a movie, so the only thing they'd find out would be whether or not you liked popcorn. So I said what a great idea!

My jeans got dirty just getting into the canoe, never mind sitting down. And I needn't have wasted so much time worrying about what top I was going to wear, since we had to put on what Connor calls personal flotation devices (and I call life jackets). I looked like a bright blue marshmallow. (I could've been on a date with Dolittle!) And then I got really, *really* nervous. The way I would if I had to talk in front of the whole school. Not because of the canoe (I've had enough near-death experiences because of Zelda not to let that kind of thing bother me). Because of him. Just being near him made me feel fizzy.

And it wasn't because he's even better looking than I remembered, or even because of that smile (which, if you ask me, should be registered as a lethal weapon). I never really tried to impress a boy before. I've never had to. They're either my friends or they don't really know I'm there. But I wanted to impress Connor. I wanted him to remember all the intelligent, funny, and interesting things I said. It made me a wreck. You know how when you're anxious you can hear your heart beating? I could hear my heart beating *and* my breathing *and* the blood moving in my arteries and veins. I swear I could even feel dead skin flaking off. (Wait till I tell Sunia. I've spent two years in yoga class trying to become aware of every part of my body, when all I had to do was get in a small boat with Connor Bowden. I could've saved a fortune!) So instead of being intelligent, funny, and interesting, I pretty much just sat there like a sack of potatoes. I couldn't even think of something *not* clever to say. So he did most of the talking, and I did most of the smiling and nodding. Every time he made a joke, I laughed. I sounded like I was in a who-can-laugh-the-most contest. It was agony. I could see that my whole life was going to be like this. Forever. There really was a curse on me. I'd have one disastrous date every year or two. Until even I got tired of trying. And then I'd end up living with a whole bunch of cats and a Weimaraner like Gran's friend, Aviva. I guess my hands were really sweaty or I wasn't concentrating enough or something, but all of a sudden I dropped my paddle. We both made a grab for it. We banged heads. We slammed shoulders. We capsized the canoe. But besides all his other terrific qualities, Connor is really calm. (Unlike anyone I'm related to.) There was no panic. No screaming. He told me what to do like he was telling me the time. We weren't too far out, so we grabbed the rim and swam the canoe back to shore. When we got on dry land, Connor said, "Boy, some people will do anything to keep cool." We both thought that was hilarious. And I said it must be something that runs in my family, because my sister capsized a rowboat last summer. We cracked up again. And that was it! After that I wasn't nervous at all. By the time we got to his house we were practically dry, so we sat out on the porch and talked and talked and talked. We talked about all kinds of things, not just the normal stuff like what your favorite music is and what things you think are cool. We talked about what we really like and really don't like. About embarrassing stuff that's happened to us. Things we worry about. Things that really make us mad. I didn't expect it to be like that. I expected it to be about liking dogs and salt-and-vinegar potato chips, and hating violent movies (which he does!). It was pretty intense.

But in a good way. We laughed a lot, too. (Besides being smart, he's also very funny.) Later we went down to the Snack Shack for crab cakes and fries. Connor said it was the best date he'd ever had. I said me too. (But I didn't say it was more or less the only one.) And then he kissed me. Since nobody's ever tried to kiss me before, I didn't actually have a first-date policy in place. I kind of froze. Connor asked what was wrong. So I said I've never really done much kissing before. He said that was OK; practice makes perfect! And he kissed me again.

When I got home Mom wanted to know how my date went. I said it was OK. Then she wanted to know what happened to my jeans. She said I looked like I fell in the lake.

I have to try to sleep. I've been talking to Nomi for so long my throat's sore.

FRIDAY

Zelda wanted to know what was wrong with my lips. I said they got chapped being out on the lake. Gus smirked at me over her coffee, but instead of annoying me like it usually would, it made me feel kind of grown up. As if I belong to a special club. The Girls Who Are Kissed Club!

I couldn't believe what a good mood I was in today. Despite my family, thinking I would never have a real date, and sleeping in the pantry, I'm usually a pretty happy person. But today I was *really* happy. I felt like all the good things I could think of had happened at once. I ask you, how can nearly drowning, a few hours of talking, a couple of crab cakes, and a crash course in kissing make a person feel like this? I don't know. I really don't. But it's as if I have some amazing secret—like the meaning of life or something like that. Something that makes everything really fantastic. Nomi says it's just endorphins. (Which are peptides, not marine mammals.) She says I could get the same effect running four miles, hanging off a cliff, or eating a bag of chilis. (I know which option I'd take.) I said there's such a thing as being too practical. But nothing could dump on my good mood. Not Gus starting a fight about the orange juice. Not being late for work because Zelda wouldn't leave the house. Not my hair frizzing up in the humidity. Nothing. Not even when Broccoli Man did that thing where he won't get out of the car, roll down the window, or speak, but still wants to be served. I didn't lose my cheery smile for even a second. I pointed to every vegetable individually. And when I had to guess how much Broccoli Man wanted, did I sigh and groan and say I'd had enough and that if he didn't stop he was going to be banned again? No, I did not. In fact, Green Pickup Guy commented that I looked like I was singing, even though I was just weighing vegetables. Finally Ely noticed. "What happened?" he asked. "Your sisters move out?" I should be so lucky. I said nothing happened; I was just in a good mood. It's one thing telling Nomi about Connor, but I don't want to jinx things by blabbing about him when we've only had one date. (Even if it was the best date he ever had.)

*   *   *

And then Connor called me at work today! He said he'd tried to text me and get me on the landline last night to make sure I hadn't come down with pneumonia after being dumped in the lake, but he couldn't get through. He thought there was something wrong with my phones. How cute is that? I said I was talking to Nomi and charging my cell. He said I should charge my cell while I'm sleeping so people can get through to me when I'm awake. Then he wanted to know what I was doing right then. I told him I was filling baskets with tomatoes. He has a baseball game tonight, but he wanted to know if I wanted to do something on Saturday. I said yes. When we hung up, Ely was standing there staring at me. I said, "What? Are my pointy ears showing or something?" Ely said, "No, but I think maybe your nose is starting to grow."

Nomi says it's unprecedented for a guy to call you the same night you went out with him. She said she heard somewhere that it's three days minimum, because they like to seem cool. I said what, they have a manual? She said yes. I said didn't I tell you he's not like most guys? She said, "Yes, you did, Hildy. Several times."

Louie came over after supper. He wanted to know why I missed Movie Club yesterday. It wasn't like I didn't tell him I couldn't make it. I texted him from the Snack Shack. I said I told you, I was busy. Louie said yeah, I got that part. But busy doing what? I didn't know he was counting, but Louie says I've never missed a single Movie Club since we started it. Not even that time I twisted my ankle and couldn't walk (Louie and Jax carried me over). I said well, if you *must* know, I had a date and it went on longer than I thought it would. Louie didn't seem to think me having a date was a freak event worthy of fireworks and a commemorative poem. He said that I should've brought him with me. As if! I want Connor to get to know me before he gets to know my friends. (I figure meeting somebody's friends is kind of like looking in their closet or the medicine cabinet. It could put you off in a serious way.) I said, "Oh, sure, and then Scorsese corners him in the hall or won't let him out of the bathroom and you put it on YouTube. That should win me points." Then we started listing all the other things Scorsese might do. (He wouldn't really hurt anyone; he's all bark and growl, but he is a schnauzer, so he's fairly insane—he once treed the UPS man, and now they won't deliver to the Masiados anymore, not even at Christmas.) When we finally stopped laughing, we played Scrabble. Louie left just as this massive thunderstorm started. We stood on the porch for a few minutes watching it, but then we could hear Scorsese and Hitchcock going nuts (they hate thunder), so Louie ran home to calm them down and I went to check on Zelda because she's afraid of thunderstorms (that and teaspoons, et cetera, et cetera, et cetera . . .) but she was sleeping through this one.

Find myself thinking a lot about Connor. I can't see any major flaws in him. Smart. Funny. Good-looking. Sensitive. Sweet. (Nomi says if you think a person's totally perfect, it's only because you don't know them well enough. But Nomi can be immensely cynical for someone who looks as if she must always've played the angel in school plays.) So then I was thinking about some of my favorite movies and wondering if Connor likes them too. And what he'd think of the sock-shaped cookie jar I made my mom for Christmas (it's my best piece so far). Or if he eats duck or okra (which would bring him down by at least half a point from a perfect ten). Stuff like that. It's weird. I don't know if all that means I have a major crush on Connor or if I'm just relieved not to be the only one of my girlfriends not seeing anyone. I mean, it could happen. That we're seeing each other. I know we haven't had our second date yet, but we're going to. He said so. So who knows . . . ? It's the most exciting thing that's happened to me since the blackout last winter. Maybe pretty soon when someone asks me what I'm doing on the weekend, I can say (casual as a pair of slippers), "Oh, I'm going out with my boyfriend."

OMG, I just realized! Now I have to find something else to wear tomorrow night. No wonder everybody says girls are obsessed with clothes. But I ask you, do we have a choice? No, we do not.

Gus says now might be a good time to stock up on lip balm. I've waited seventeen years for Gus to give me some big-sisterly advice, and that's what it is. Lip balm. Can't wait to hear what she says after the next seventeen years.

SATURDAY

I am going out with the most thoughtful and considerate boy on the Eastern Seaboard (or possibly the entire continent). Connor texted me at work today to remind me that we had a date tonight. (Um, duh. I'm more likely to forget where I live.) And also to tell me that he thought about it a lot and decided tonight's going to be a Have a Normal Night Out Without Danger of Drowning Date. (How cute is that?) He thought we could go to the multiplex at the shopping plaza. Nomi says getting in touch two days running *and* reminding me that we have a date is unprecedented, too. She says the only time Jax has ever reminded her about anything was when she borrowed his black hoodie and he wanted to make sure she returned it. She figures Connor definitely hasn't read the *How to Be a Guy* manual. Either that or he just landed from another planet. Maybe he's really a two-foot-tall alien with gold skin, a head like an enormous egg, and eyes like swimming holes, who can change the course of rivers by moving one finger and read minds. (Would it bother me if he was? Not if he keeps his human form.)

So anyway, we were more than an hour early for the movie. Connor said he figured he got the time wrong because he couldn't wait to see me again. (It's just as well I'm made of flesh and blood and not ice, or I would've turned into a puddle.) While we waited we went to Chez Danielle, which is meant to be like an outdoor café in Paris (except not outdoors, and not in Paris) for an iced tea (Connor's gone off coffee since he's been working at the café—like Uncle

Nick went off meat after he worked in a slaughterhouse one summer). We talked so much that we forgot about the movie! We got into some *real* personal stuff. I told him about my crazy family. How they're all so full-on and dramatic all the time. He wanted to know if I meant that my parents are actors. I said no, my dad's a mechanic and my mom knits socks. But my mom's part Greek and part Spanish, and my dad's Italian, so they have the Mediterranean shouters' and arm-wavers' gene pools covered. My parents think having an argument is the same as having a conversation. And even though my sisters are completely different, they're both it's-a-one-girl-world types. You know, the universe starts HERE. (And ends HERE, too.) Zelda's like that because she has a syndrome, and Gus is like that because she *is* a syndrome. They make everything into a crisis. It doesn't rain; it's a monsoon. You don't have a cold; you have pneumonia. You don't run out of cereal; you ruin your life. Which is probably why I'm the exact opposite. I'm the calm, steady, quiet, low-maintenance, dependable one. So I'm kind of overlooked most of the time. Connor said NOT BY HIM. (How sweet can you get?) And he told me about his family. They're not crazy at all. They're all calm and civilized and reasonable. Connor's dad's a lawyer and his mom's a realtor. They both work a lot, especially his dad. He says he's never heard them have a fight.

Not a real, shaking-the-glasses, hurling-the-nearest-small-object-across-the-room kind of fight. (You can bet Connor's mother never locked Connor's father out of the house.) He says they don't really do emotions. But they're OK; they're parents. They have a lot of expectations. And they can be really critical. I said it's their job to be critical. It's in their contract. I've seen it: Clause 58b. He laughed, but then he said they don't criticize his brother Cal the way they do him. They think Cal's perfect. Even though Cal doesn't live at home anymore, they still talk about how wonderful he is all the time. It made me feel kind of sad for Connor. (At least my parents know none of their children is perfect.) When he dropped me off, he said that was the best date he ever had. I said that's what you said last time. He said, "Exactly. I can't wait till the next one." And the kissing's already getting *way* better. I know I have nothing to compare it to, but electricity definitely seems to be involved.

The parents were watching a movie in the living room when I got home. My mom wanted to know how my date was. I said good. She said, "Well, that's an improvement." My dad wanted to know when he was going to "meet this young man." I said he's not helping you with the deck, if that's what you think.

*   *   *

Nomi said she figures the only way Jax would miss a movie to talk would be if he ran into a bunch of blues musicians in the mall. He certainly wouldn't miss one to talk to *her*. She wanted to know when she's going to be officially introduced to Mr. Coffee. I swear, she sounded like my father. I said you know, I've only known him a week. You could give us a chance to see if we're going to know each other for two weeks before you meet him. She said, "Don't look now, Hildegard, but you're entering week number two." I said I'll let her know when I think Connor's ready.

Here's a historic first: Gus is right. I'm definitely going to need more lip balm.

SUNDAY

Went to see Aunt Lonnie and Uncle Grant for the big barbecue today like we do every Fourth of July. The Fourth is usually my best holiday, because I get to hang out with my cousins and there's tons for us to do. (OK, I admit it, I was also kind of looking forward to casually mentioning Connor, since I was the only one over twelve who'd never had a date.) And I get to see my aunts and uncles, who are the best and longest-running sitcom in the history of the world. But this year I was kind of preoccupied. With Connor Bowden—even though he wasn't there. He was at his family's barbecue, but his cousins are all a lot younger, so he had no one to talk to. He said it could only be more boring if they were all speaking Russian. Connor said that if the Founding Fathers had had any idea that their revolution would lead to him having to hear his Uncle Todd's lecture on why he should study architecture every Fourth of July, they might have reconsidered separating from England. He said thank God he had me to text or he might lose his mind. Aunt Suze wanted to know who was calling me every two minutes. I said I didn't know she was timing me. She said, "So who is it, Hildy?" (The D'Angelos have never produced any diplomats, and Aunt Suze's in no danger of ruining that record.) I said it was just a friend. Naturally, as soon as I said "just a friend," my entire family (including Gran, who is absolutely old enough to know better) shouted, "Hildy has a boyfriend!" Uncle Nick said he hoped this boyfriend was paying my phone bill. Naturally the girls wanted to know all about him, but I was too busy texting back to say much then.

After lunch the men went to play bocce and everybody else went down to the lake, but I stayed up on the deck talking to Connor. So I missed the day's big drama. According to eyewitness accounts, it was even better than when Uncle Enzo threw his hamburger at Uncle Ed (and then they had an actual fistfight and Gran threw a pitcher of iced tea over them to break it up—it was immense). Our cousin Paola decided Gus was flirting with her boyfriend, and so she pushed Gus in the lake. (Probably we shouldn't have any family occasions where there's a body of water involved.) Then Gus charged out of the lake like a really annoyed Loch Ness Monster (description by Zelda D'Angelo) and pulled Paola in. Then Paola tried to drown Gus. It was Del, Paola's boyfriend, who separated them. They both took a punch at him when they got to dry land. The uncles kept playing their game through all this turmoil (they would only stop if enemy tanks came rolling across the lawn), but the aunts jumped up and down and shrieked and wrung their hands (except my mom, because she was too busy shielding Zelda from being splashed—if any water got on her, you would've heard some real screaming). Gran said it made her feel young again (I wouldn't dare ask!). We left after that, because it was Paola's house and she wasn't going anywhere.

Connor said since it was a holiday we should have A Night Under the Stars tonight. I didn't see how we could do that when I was in Redbank and he was all the way over in Milton. He said we might be a hundred miles apart, but we were looking up at the same stars, weren't we? (How romantic is *that*?) So he sat on his grandparents' deck and I sat near the construction site that's our deck. It was really cool. Wound up talking for ages. He asked me about *all my other boyfriends*! He didn't believe me at first when I said I hadn't had any. (Because I'm so wonderful!) I told him about my two and a half dates. That made him laugh. So then I said I figured he must've had a few girlfriends. He said he's never had much luck with girls. *Until now.* The sky was crammed with so many stars, it was as if God was trying to see how many He could fit in. It was really romantic. Like we were on an ocean liner together or in a spaceship. I almost felt as if I could reach out and hold his hand. I was floating through the cosmos like a dream. And then I heard a toilet flush. I said, "Where are you, Connor?" He was in the bathroom. I said I thought we were sharing a tender moment gazing at the stars. He said we were. He could see them from the bathroom window.

MONDAY

Connor doesn't get back till Wednesday night because every summer over the Fourth and on Labor Day weekend he goes fishing with his dad and his grandfather. It's a Bowden men tradition. They have pioneer ancestors. The fishing meant we were out of communication the whole day. I kept thinking I'd lost my phone.

Lenora's still banned from the Palacio pool, so Nomi and I went to Cristina's this afternoon. Asked Cristina if she misses Max a lot. She said not so you'd notice. She talks to him every couple of nights unless they're all singing songs around the campfire or someone sets off a stink bomb in the bunkhouse or something like that. And anyway if she wants to fight with someone, she has her sister. Nomi says Jax's never gone away long enough for her to miss him. It's weird. I know I only just met Connor, but not being able to talk to him all day made me feel kind of lonely. Told Nomi when we were walking home. She says I'll get over it. She says it's like when you get a new pair of shoes and at first you're so careful with them you clean them every time you wear them. But soon the only time you clean them is when you step in muck. I said she's such a romantic I may start calling her Cupid.

TUESDAY

Mr. Kitosky's still away, so we all went bowling tonight, including Grady (I should stop saying stuff like "including Grady." He's definitely part of the Mob now). I had them all in stitches over Paola shoving Gus in the lake. (Think how much funnier it would've been if I'd actually *seen* it and didn't have to rely on what Gran and Zelda told me.) Cristina wanted to know if Gus really was flirting with Paola's boyfriend. I said, "Only in his dreams." Believe me, of the two of them, Del isn't the one who's stun-gun gorgeous. Besides, I know my sister. She doesn't go after other people's boyfriends; she has plenty of her own. There aren't any cell phones allowed in the alley, because a sudden burst of music could throw off someone's game (which is why Mr. Kitosky pushed Mr. Ledbetter that time—his phone was playing "My Way" at top volume), so it wasn't till I got home that I saw there was a text from Connor. It said: *SIX BIG ONES!* It took me a minute to realize he meant fish.

WEDNESDAY

Ely showed up at the stand today dressed as the Vegetable Avenger. The Vegetable Avenger rights wrongs to the Vegetable Kingdom. He turns back pesticides, saves organic farms from being contaminated by GM seeds, rescues plants from polluted land and water, and is the enemy of industrial farming. Ely was wearing green leggings (at least the heat wave finally broke—otherwise he would've had to paint his legs), this orange smock thing of his mom's, and a green paper bag with crêpe-paper fronds glued to it. So basically he was a carrot. I said if only I'd known, I would have come as celery. He said, "Then we could go to the beach for a dip!" I said you know, nobody'd believe you're in college. Choked, we were laughing so much.

Connor texted me at least six times at work today! There's a big baseball game tomorrow afternoon and he wants me to go, to bring him and the team luck. Swapped my shift with Mike again.

Ely said if I spend much more time with my head bent over my phone, he's going to forget what I look like. Ran out of charge around 4:30. Ely got on his knees to thank the gods of wireless communication just as the Countess pulled in. She wanted to know if he'd lost something. He said just some of his mind.

Had a dentist appointment this afternoon. Ely gave me a lift in his pickup. He was still dressed as the Vegetable Avenger. The Vegetable Avenger may have several superpowers, but being invisible isn't one of them. Everybody was doing double takes. You should've seen their faces. It was hilarious. There was a lot of horn honking, but not like we were blocking the road or being too slow to move when the light changed or anything like that. It was happy honking. "You see?" said Ely. "The Vegetable Avenger spreads joy wherever he goes." I said, "Joy and manure." As soon as I sat down in the chair, Dr. Croxley wanted to know if he really saw me pull up in a truck driven by a root vegetable. I said, "Yes."

Worked with Louie on the epic saga of *Love and Lawn Mowing* tonight. I thought he was literally going to split his sides when I told him about the Vegetable Avenger. Naturally, Louie wants to film Ely. He figures he can make it a series. I said yeah, *Killer Carrots Take Over the World*. Then he wanted to know if I was bringing What's-His-Name to Movie Club this week. I said we couldn't make it because of the game. Louie said, "Since when do you like baseball?" I said I don't know whether I like it or not, do I? I've never actually sat through a whole game. Louie said, "Maybe there's a reason for that."

There were three messages from Connor when I got back to Casa D'Angelo. One when he was almost home. One when he got home. And one after he had a shower. (I don't even have to ask Nomi to know how UNPRECEDENTED that is!) I called him right back. He wanted to know what was up. He'd left three messages. I said I was charging my phone. He said he really wishes I'd charge it while I'm sleeping. He likes to be able to reach me. I said that if he always has to be able to reach me, it's going to be a little hard for me to bungee jump off the Empire State Building or speak in front of the United Nations. He thought that was hilarious.

THURSDAY

Connor came to pick me up. I'd been keeping watch because I wanted to get out the door before my mom knew he was here, but Zelda distracted me by suddenly dumping everything in my bag on the floor. Anyway, I think my mom must've spotted him even before he got out of the car. By the time I got to them, they were old friends. She told us to have a good time, and she told him to drive carefully. It was excruciating. But Connor just smiled and said, "I always drive carefully, Mrs. D'Angelo. You don't have to worry about that." And then she invited him to supper. Tomorrow! I almost fell off the porch. All I could think was she *had* to be kidding. She was inviting him to EAT WITH US? Was she trying to stop him from ever seeing me again? Fortunately, Connor's doing extra shifts to make up for the days he lost killing fish, so he can't do tomorrow. What a shame! But just as I started to relax, my mother said, "Well, what about next Friday?" I tried to tug Connor backward, willing him to say, *I'm really sorry, but I'm busy that night, too.* He said, "That'd be great. Thank you, Mrs. D'Angelo. I'd love to come." Which was when I did fall off the porch. I tripped over Mrs. Claws. When we got in the car, I was going to tell him that he didn't have to come to supper just to be polite—I could make up some story about how he'd been infected by a virulent disease he'd contracted from coffee beans—but before I could open my mouth, he handed me something wrapped in Christmas paper. (It was all he could find.) Inside was a crystal in the shape of a star to hang from my window. It was to say sorry for the other night when he flushed the toilet in the middle of our romantic space odyssey. HOW CUTE IS THAT?

I'm going to be honest. If we're talking about sports, as far as baseball goes, I'd probably rather watch gymnastics. (And if we're talking just in general, I'd rather watch a movie. Even one the guys picked.) But that doesn't mean that I didn't enjoy the game, because I did. It couldn't fail, really. What was I going to do, read a book while Connor was playing? Fall asleep? Go sit in the car? Yeah, right. And next week I'm climbing Mount Everest dressed as Minnie Mouse. I couldn't take my eyes off the field. And who was that girl bouncing up and down on her bench and screaming louder than anybody else? It was me! (Luckily Mom sometimes watches baseball on TV, so I had an idea of what was happening.) You know what else? I really did bring them luck. Connor scored two runs, and his team (the Smashers or the Crashers or the Bashers — something like that) won for the first time all season. You should've seen how happy Connor was. Afterward we went with some of the team (Stu, JC, Albie, and Milt) for pizza. I was the only girl, which was kind of weird because I just sat there smiling and nodding and acting like a silent echo. (It wouldn't have been weird if they were my guys, because my guys think of me as a person. But these guys seemed to think of me as the girl with Connor, so they didn't really talk to me. All they talked about was the Game, which is a lot less interesting than watching it.) Connor said he could tell they really liked me. I said, "Can you tell that I really like you?" I couldn't believe I said that. Thank God we were sitting in the car, and he couldn't see me turn the color of Farmer John's tomatoes. I mean, where did that come from? I've never said anything like that before in my life. I've never even thought of saying anything like that. But you know what he said? He said: CAN *YOU*?

Went into the kitchen to get some water. Dad was fixing himself a snack. He wanted to know how the game went. I got a text while we were talking. Dad said, "Don't tell me that's *him*." I said he just wanted to say good night. Dad said he thought we did that in the car. We were there long enough to say good night to the entire East Coast. I took the opportunity to beg him not to make dumb jokes when Connor comes to supper. He said he wouldn't dream of it. Then he said the best thing about Connor coming to dinner is that at least that'll be one night when he won't be texting me all the time. Doom looms.

I always figured that if somebody stuck his tongue in my mouth it would be revolting. But it isn't.

FRIDAY

Because I changed my shift again, Farmer John wanted to know if I was playing musical chairs (only without the music and without the chairs). Ely said, "So what's going on? You're jumping around like a rabbit." So I broke down and told him about Connor. "First boyfriend," said Ely. "No wonder you keep dropping the vegetables and giving people the wrong change." He wanted to know all about him. How we met. Where he lives. What he's like. I said, "What are you, an honorary girl? I thought boys didn't get into that stuff." He said he wanted to make sure Connor's good enough for me. He thinks of me as his kid sister. I said maybe he should think of me as somebody else's kid sister.

Nomi came by the stand today with the two little kids she babysits. She was hoping to see Ely dressed as a carrot, but he was just dressed as a boy. She said everybody wanted to know where I was last night. I was where I told them I'd be. I couldn't very well not go to Connor's game, could I? Nomi said wait till you've sat through half a dozen of them and the three-hour instant replay that happens after the game when the guys all hang out together. Then you'll jump at any excuse — hang gliding for charity, a kangaroo hunt, plastic surgery, absolutely anything — to avoid having to sit through another one. I pointed out that there are millions of people in the world who are crazy about ball games. Nomi said, "Yeah, but you're not one of them." I said it's all right for her to be jaded and cynical, but this is all new to me. And anyway, how does she know? Jax is the guy they invented bleachers for. She said, "But he's a guitar freak, isn't he? It boils down to the same thing." She used to go with him every time he was having a musical moment with his friends. And she's spent hours of her life sitting in a room listening to him practice. At first she thought it was really cool, but after a while it was more like a radio you can't turn off. Nomi said she knows more about chord changes, dead blues musicians, and how to tune a guitar than any person whose total musical ability consists of being able to turn on a stereo should.

.

Louie's parents had their mah-jongg gang over tonight. Louie says the sound of the tiles slapping on the table drives him nuts. He can even hear it in his studio. So he came over to bask in the peace and quiet that is Casa D'Angelo. (Everything's relative, isn't it?) The parents were arguing over what they were going to watch on TV. We went into the kitchen to play Clue with Zelda. Zelda takes forever with her turn and everybody else's (this is why no one's ever going to teach her chess), but that was cool because it meant Louie and I could talk. When Connor got home from work, he called me. I answered on a laugh. He wanted to know what I was laughing about. I said Louie'd been telling me a funny story. Connor said he didn't know I was busy. I started to explain that we weren't busy like we were just about to climb into the space shuttle; we were only hanging out and playing Clue with Zelda, but he said he'd call me later and hung up. Louie looked at me as if he was framing a shot. I said we'd lost the signal, and I'd just be a minute. I wanted to call Connor back. Went outside for privacy. I said, "Are you OK?" He said he was pretty wiped out from a double shift of sprinkling chocolate on foam and saying "Have a nice day!" Connor said there are times when he thinks he may never smile again. Then I asked him why he hung up on me like that. He said he hadn't. He just didn't want to bother me when I was busy. I said I was playing a dumb game, not teeing off in the Open. Zelda's going to win, because even if she didn't cheat, we'd let her win, so it's not like he was disrupting the tension of the game. By the time I got back, Zelda was watching TV with Mom and Louie and my dad had started a game of chess.

SATURDAY

Things were all normal, fill-the-baskets, bag-the-potatoes routine at work today till Green Pickup Guy showed up and Ely added to the series of humiliations that dot my life like greenfly on kale by telling him I have a boyfriend! This was all because Green Pickup Guy said he was surprised to see me on a Saturday, and Ely said, *Scarlett's got a boyfriend, so her schedule keeps changing.* Never mind the ground opening up and swallowing *me;* if it had opened up, I would've pushed Ely in.

Was supposed to see Connor tonight, but his car wouldn't start when he got out of work, so he had to be towed to his dad's mechanic. Both of his parents were out, so it was hours before he finally got home. Jax was dragged off to Florida on a family vacation (Florida! In July! As Nomi said, why did his folks bother having him if they're trying to kill him?), so Nomi came over and we fooled around with makeup and different hairstyles and talked about life and ate pretzels and drank iced tea. Nomi said it really is epic how often Connor phones and texts me. She says there've been weekends at Casa Slevka when the only words her parents exchanged were "What's for supper?" and "Did you put the garbage out?"

SUNDAY

Went to yoga. Cristina, Maggie, and Sara were also impressed by how much Connor talks to me. Cristina says she's talked more to Max since he's been at Camp Caribou than she has in all the time she's known him. Which is only because he's stuck with a bunch of little kids who tell fart jokes all day and is starved for normal human companionship. Maggie says Grady talks to her in person, but he only uses the phone to impart information. Yes. No. Seven o'clock. That kind of thing. Sara says Kruger'll talk about the band and any other band he can think of and music, but if you ask him about anything else, his usual response is either "yeah," "um," or "whatever." After yoga they were all going to go swimming at Cristina's. I said I couldn't because I promised Connor I'd drop by the mall, since I've barely seen him all week. That got a lot of *oohing* and girlish giggling. And then they all started harassing me about when they were going to meet him. I said I'd only just met him myself. In case I forgot how to count, Maggie said I met him two weeks ago. Cristina said she's heard of marriages that didn't last that long. The next thing I knew, they'd all decided to come along. (God forbid they should ask *my* opinion.) Cristina said she'd been meaning to take that skirt back (again). Sara said she might as well start looking for a birthday present for her mom. "Any excuse to shop," said Maggie. Nomi said, "Well, I'm not staying home by myself!" I knew they just wanted to check out Connor, but I didn't really mind. I wanted to show him off. And they're going to meet him sometime.

The mall was so busy, you would've thought it was Christmas (only without the decorations and nobody was wearing big coats or trapper hats or singing "Rudolph the Red-Nosed Reindeer"). We took Cristina's skirt back and went to a couple of stores that were having sales, and then we went over to Café Olé! We all went to the counter to do the ordering. Before I could even open my mouth to say hi or introduce them, Nomi said to Connor, "Hi, I'm Nomi. I saw you before? The day you met Hildy? I've heard *all* about you, but we've never actually met. Officially." She made it sound like she'd read his autobiography and seen the movie. And to make it worse, Cristina, Maggie, and Sara were kind of swaying together and nodding. It was definitely a major open-up-floor-and-let-me-in moment. For me. But Connor took it in his stride, I guess because he's used to dealing with people. He just smiled like he wanted them to have a nice day. To stop them from yakking and making him think they knew everything about him including his shoe size, I did the introductions. Loudly. "And this is Sara, Maggie, and Cristina. You saw them, too. And I told you all about them. Remember?" Connor was the only one who didn't giggle (except me). "I hope it wasn't all bad," said Maggie. "Don't believe a word she says," said Cristina. "It's all lies. We're really very nice." Sara said, "Hi. I'm the drummer." Connor repeated their names and nodded and said hi and gave them his special melt-your-heart smile. He took our orders and started filling cups while the four of them leaned against the counter, talking as if they were being paid by the word. I was so relieved when we got our drinks that I practically ran to the table. "For God's sake,"

I said, "you're acting like a bunch of tweenies. We're the future doctors, physicists, and mothers of America. Can't you show some maturity and dignity?" Nomi said I forgot to mention lap dancers, waitresses, and cleaning ladies. They all thought that was one of the most hilarious things they'd ever heard. I turned to Nomi. "And you," I said. "Why did you say you'd heard a lot about him like that? He'll think I do nothing but talk about him." She pretended to look all shocked and surprised. "You don't?" Cue more hilarity. But then they finally settled down and we started playing one of our mall games—the one where you try to guess what people have in their shopping bags—and that distracted them from Connor for a while. I was a little worried, because it wasn't like he was expecting a major visitation, and I didn't want to overwhelm him. Or annoy him. I kept glancing over and smiling at Connor to reassure him. And he kept glancing over and smiling back, so I figured it was OK. When I went up to say good-bye, he said, "What about trying for that movie tonight?" And then HE KISSED ME IN FRONT OF EVERYBODY. Just like that! In Café Olé! It was dry and quick, but it was wonderful. When we left the café, Nomi said, "So I take it you two are officially a couple." I can't believe it myself.

*   *   *

Saw Blue Eye-Shadow Lady when we were waiting in line outside the multiplex. It took me a minute to recognize her because I've never seen her away from the farm stand before. She looked different without a head of cabbage in her hands. Connor wanted to know who I was staring at. That's when she saw me and waved and I realized who she was. I said it was Blue Eye-Shadow Lady and waved back. He said I had good eyes if I could tell what color eye shadow she was wearing from there.

The movie was OK. What I remember of it. I guess I wasn't paying that much attention. Afterward we sat in the car and talked a lot about things we're going to do. He wants to teach me how to play backgammon. And take me sailing. And show me this secret beach he found. And take me hiking. And make me a CD of his favorite songs. And I'm going to make him a mug. And maybe teach him some yoga. And . . . EVERYTHING! He says he's never known anybody like me before. (How sweet is that?)

Asked Connor what he thought of my friends. He didn't remember them from before at all. He said they seemed OK, but he didn't say it with a lot of enthusiasm. I said you don't like them? He said they were a little in-your-face. And loud. And they never stopped smiling. I said they were nervous. They're not always like that. He said no, I figured they must sleep sometime. We both laughed.

Told Nomi what Connor said about never knowing anybody like me before. She didn't understand what a romantic thing that was to say to someone. She got all serious and niggling the way she does. She said she thought we agreed that every person in the world is unique. I said we did. Every person *is* unique. She said so then whenever you meet someone new, no matter who it is, you've never met anyone like that person before. I said what are you, my sister? Can't you let me be happy for ten minutes? She said she was only saying. I asked her where she thought she was when they were handing out the romance gene. She said she was probably scrubbing out the toilet bowl.

I used to be afraid of kissing. Not afraid, exactly, but, you know, I didn't really get it. When you see people doing it in a movie, it looks like they're trying to bend each other's teeth back. Or maybe shove something into the other person's mouth without using hands. I figured they throw in the kissing in movies when they can't think of anything else to do. Boy, was I ever wrong. It's just boring to watch. And I'm improving in increments of at least a hundred.

MONDAY

In a state of bliss all day. I have a boyfriend! I not only have a boyfriend; I have a fantastic, immense, awesome, impossibly wonderful boyfriend. How did this happen? Two weeks and two days ago, I thought I was going to be the only girl in my class to graduate high school without ever being kissed. Even worse, I was looking at a future of frozen dinners for one and a lot of pets. And now look at me! It's incredible how happy a person can be.

Nomi says you can't base your personal happiness on someone else. It has to come from within. Sometimes I want to put her in a plane that's going to somewhere really far away.

TUESDAY

Farmer John said business was definitely up when Ely dressed as the Vegetable Avenger. He wants Ely to do it again. Not every day, but maybe once a week. So it's something people talk about and look forward to. And tell their friends about. Ely wants me to do it with him. He has it all figured out. I just have to wear something green and glue some paper leaves onto a swimming cap, and I'll be the Vegetable Avenger's trusty sidekick, Lethal Lettuce. I said I'll think about it.

Connor's started texting me every hour or so. Just *hi* ☺ or *thnkng bout u* or *i really hate coffee* or *boy do I wish u wr hr.* And sometimes he calls when he's on his break. Especially if something funny happened. Every time my phone went, Ely said, "Geewillikers, I wonder who that could be."

* * *

Maggie's mom stopped by the stand today for tomatoes. And just happened to mention that she just happened to hear that I'm seeing someone. That's exactly what she said, with a big smile: "So, Hildy, I hear you're seeing someone." (Oh, those jungle drums, they just never stop, do they? Day and night. Night and day. *Boomboomboomboomboom.*) But I wasn't really annoyed. I was kind of pleased, to be honest. I don't usually do things people talk about. (Except stuff like the time I threw up in the middle of the third-grade Christmas play. Which wasn't something I did, really. It was something that happened.) I joked with Ely that maybe I should take an ad out in the *Redbank Observer,* you know, in case there's anybody in town who hasn't heard about me and Connor. Ely said I can save my money—he's already posted it on Facebook. (If I didn't know he hates Facebook, I would've thrown a tomato at him.) He wanted to know why Connor texts me so much. Ely says it's as if he doesn't want me to be by myself. I said Connor just likes to keep in touch, that's all. Ely said he likes plums, but he doesn't eat one every ten minutes.

Broccoli Man called the stand to say that he couldn't leave the house but he needed some things. This happens once a month or so. (I think of it as the stand's period:

annoying, inconvenient, but just the way things work.) Sometimes he can't leave home because there are too many people outside or "the numbers are wrong." Sometimes it's because THEY are waiting for him or he doesn't like the weather. I didn't ask. There's such a thing as too much information. So Ely gave me a ride home, and we dropped off Broccoli Man's order (12 ounces of string beans, 15 ounces of potatoes, 18 ounces of tomatoes, 18 ounces of squash, two bunches of spinach, one head of lettuce, *not iceberg, whatever you do!*). I had to go around the back and put everything through the cat door. Then he passed out the money. You have to wonder what his neighbors think. Ely said they probably think he's nuts.

More trauma and drama at Casa D'Angelo. The washing machine broke *again*. (It's as if we live on a tape loop.) My mother said it was my father's fault because he's too cheap to buy a new one. My father said it was working dandy as candy after he fixed it last time it broke and that he suspects outside interference. That means one of us. Escaped to the Masiados' to help Louie with the *Anniversary Waltz*. (That's what he's decided to call the *Love and Lawn Mowing* movie about his folks.) Personally, I think it should be called the *Anniversary Tango*. The waltz is very formal and orderly, which the Masiados aren't.

Almost every clip has them waving their arms around and yelling. (No wonder Louie feels so at home with my family, right?) So far my favorite scene is when Mr. Masiado is teaching Louie's mom to drive. She backed out of the driveway and straight into the garbage can. Even though there isn't any sound, I swear you can hear Mr. Masiado shouting.

Louie said he heard I'm officially going out with What's-His-Name. I said it's Connor. And it's only semi-official. He said so are we going to meet him this week? Are you coming on Thursday? I said I'd talk to Connor and let him know. Louie said that made it sound pretty official to him.

When I got home there was a small purple dinosaur (a brachiosaurus, if I'm not mistaken) hanging from the kitchen light by a string. So Dad found out why the washing machine broke again.

And three messages from Connor! Nomi wants to know why he texts me so much. I said because he's unprecedented. She said he's more like a haunting.

WEDNESDAY

Blue Eye-Shadow Lady wanted to know who the handsome young man is that she saw me with the other night. So I got to say it out loud for the first time! "He's my boyfriend." Just saying it made me feel like my heart was going to pop. She said we make a really cute couple! (How awesome is that?) Then the Countess came for her five-a-day. She said she'd heard I have a beau. She said there's nothing like young love. Ely said, "Unless you're like Romeo and Juliet and it all ends in tears." The Countess said, "Oh, it all ends in tears, anyway." I didn't want to ask.

Connor wanted to know why we call him Broccoli Man. I told him Farmer John named him. He'd come to the stand a few times after he'd been banned from the two big supermarkets and the natural-food store over in Calder, but he'd been OK. We thought he was normal.

Well, pretty normal. And then one day he came by for broccoli, and we didn't have any. He clamped his hands to his ears and started rocking back and forth, chanting, "No! No! No!" He refused to leave. Ely had to go to the store and buy a head of broccoli and sneak it in. And then I explained that Blue Eye-Shadow Lady always wears a lot of blue eye shadow. And Green Pickup Guy drives a green pickup. And the Countess isn't really a countess, but when she first came to the stand, she always wore a tiara. (Now she just wears it on special occasions.) Connor said he was almost sorry he asked.

We're missing Movie Club again. Louie's not going to be happy. Connor says it's enough to be coming to supper with my family on Friday without having to deal with meeting all my friends in the same week. He's only human. We're going to have a Watching the Sunset Night and chill instead.

Dad's making Zelda help him with the deck as punishment for the washing machine. He'll be sorry.

The brachiosaurus is still hanging over the kitchen table.

THURSDAY

The sunset-watching was *so* immense! (I have seen the sun go down before, but not like this!) We walked up the beach till we were completely alone (except for the gulls and the bugs). We sat with our arms around each other, not talking, just being there in the moment (like yoga but without the exertion or the incense). I don't think I've ever just sat and watched the sun set before like I was watching a movie. It was mystical. Really. (Connor says a sunrise is even better. It's like watching the earth being born.) We made a wish on the first star. I wouldn't tell him what I wished for, because then it wouldn't come true. Connor said he already got his wish. And then he kissed me! (If I'd been standing up, I probably would've fallen over.)

Connor was worried about what he should bring to supper tomorrow. I said, "You." He said you can't go to someone's house without bringing something. (How sweet is that?) Does my mother like flowers? Do my parents drink wine? His dad has a wine cellar, so he could bring a bottle of wine. I've never known anybody who has a wine cellar before. He said it's more like a rack, but it's a big one. Then he thought maybe he should bring something for Zelda. He wanted to know what she's into. I said, "Trouble." He said, "No, really, Hildy. Drawing? Dancing? Computer games?" Zel's actually really good at drawing, but she already has enough crayons, pencils, and paints to start her own class. Then he wanted to know about my other sister. What's Gus into? I said she's incredibly fond of boys. Connor said it's too bad his brother's in Beijing right now, or he could bring him.

I've never felt like this before. Like I'm really special. I figure it's kind of like winning one of those talent shows or an Oscar or something. Or being a princess. Nomi doesn't get it. (Now, there's a surprise. Let me pick myself up off the floor.) She says that if you think about it, feeling special because somebody says you're great is no different from feeling lousy because someone tells you you're stupid or your eyebrows are too thick or whatever. Winning a talent show doesn't make you special, and some dork telling you that you're disgusting doesn't make you a horrible person. (Is she too much or what?) I said, "I don't think you were cleaning the toilet when they were handing out the romance gene, Nome. I think you were cleaning out those big stables in Greek mythology. You know, like Hercules." Nomi said, "You mean Augean Stables." I said, "Probably with a toothbrush."

Already put Mike on red alert for next week in case there's another game on Thursday, but now Connor says it's going to be Wednesday. Which means we can go to Movie Club!

FRIDAY

I couldn't get to sleep for hours last night. I kept thinking of all the things that could go wrong with Dinner with the D'Angelos tonight. Like my mother makes something so spicy that everybody starts sweating and at least one person nearly chokes to death (probably Connor). Or Gus stays home just to annoy me and tells him about the time I got stuck on the roof. Or Zelda throws something at him (and possibly blinds him for life). Or my father calls him by somebody else's name. Multitudes of things (all of which *have* happened, of course — I don't have the imagination to make this stuff up). People always say that your family is there for you when other people aren't. But if you ask me, that's probably because once they've met your family, other people all run for safety. My only consolation was that Gran wouldn't be here. Everything my dad knows about embarrassing his children he learned from her. And besides that, she thinks because she's old she can do and say what she wants. She says it's the advantage of age. It liberates you from having to be polite and follow the rules. And as we all know, she's not just whistling "Dixie" here. This is a woman who knows no shame. Let's not forget her one-woman sit-in at the bank. Anyway, when I finally did fall asleep, I dreamed that I was locked out of the house in my underwear. Zelda was inside, but she wouldn't open the door because she didn't feel like it. Woke up late and worried. Fortunately my Sidekick-of-the-Vegetable-Avenger costume (green footless tights, green skirt, green T-shirt) was all ready. Zelda made the hat (she really is very artistic), but the leaves are variegated, because she doesn't like plain green lettuce.

*   *   *

Couldn't concentrate on anything today. Just thinking about supper rolling toward me like a runaway train. (Fortunately when you're dressed as a head of lettuce, it distracts people from the fact that you can't count, can't bag, and can't remember the price of anything.)

Connor arrived exactly on time with flowers and wine for my parents. They were really impressed. It's not something they're used to. (The only thing they ever got from any of Gus's boyfriends was a broken mailbox.) Not only did my dad shake Connor's hand and my mom thank him about six times, but when he gave Zelda a box of crayons you can use on fabric to make your own T-shirts and stuff, they both said, "Oh, isn't that nice. What a terrific present." (And not, "Are you out of your mind? It's like giving a loaded gun to a chimp." Which is what they would've said if I gave it to her.) Zelda was thrilled and begged Connor to sit next to her. (She was so well behaved, you would've thought she was somebody else.) I was really nervous at first, naturally, but we got through the meal without one tiny scene of any kind. (There are such things as miracles!) We had pasta (no chilis), which Connor said was delicious, Zelda didn't throw anything at anybody, Gus wasn't there, and my father called Connor by the right name every time. Connor listened to my mom talk about socks as if all his life he'd hoped that someday he'd meet someone who knits mismatched socks out of recycled cotton. He asked my dad about the garage and told him all about his car breaking down the other day and even asked him some real questions about pistons and carburetors (which made my dad's day, since the rest of us would only recognize a piston if it was wearing a name tag). He had Zelda show him a few hundred of her pictures and cartoons, and then he gave her a lesson in how to draw a dragon (which made her day, since the rest of us ignore her as much as we can). He wanted to know why there's a purple dinosaur hanging from the light over the table, and when my mom said to teach the other dinosaurs a lesson, he said now he knew where I get my sense of humor. Connor thinks I have a great sense of humor. I think he's a great kisser. He said I'm not so bad myself. (Practice really does make perfect!)

He called me when he got home to say good night and to ask me to thank my parents again for having him over. I said he could ease off the clutch; they'd already said what good manners he has. So now if someone tells them he's really the leader of a motorcycle gang and carries a knife in his boot, they'll never believe it. He said they made a good impression on him too. Maybe there is something to Nomi's theory that if you think somebody's OK it's because you don't know them well enough. (Except for Connor, of course.)

Connor's folks are going out tomorrow night, so we can sit out on the deck and look at the stars together for real this time. (That is *really* sweet!)

Called Nomi to tell her how Dinner with the D'Angelos went. She couldn't believe there wasn't a single argument, tantrum, or slamming door all evening. (She's had dinner here.) I said me too. I was amazed nobody called the cops because it was so quiet they thought something horrible must've happened to us.

SATURDAY

Had a message from Connor when I turned on my phone this morning: *Gd mrng! cn't w8 2 c u 2nite!* (How cute is *that*?) Texted back: *Me 2!* My mom wanted to know why he texts me so much. I said, "You know . . ." She said she doesn't. She said it would drive her crazy if my father didn't give her any space. I said Connor gives me space. She said, "But he always seems to be in it." Went to pottery. It's been two weeks! I felt like I'd just gotten back from a long trip. Which I guess I have, if you think about it. I've been in Connor Country, having such a good time that I never missed home. Until I walked into the studio. Everybody was really happy to see me. Mrs. Chimurro said that they figured either I was sick or I'd been given an apprenticeship with a Japanese master and had abandoned them. So I told them that I'd started seeing someone and everything had gotten kind of caught up. They all said it was about time! (Romance lives in

Mrs. Chimurro's Saturday class. Probably because Nomi Slevka isn't in it.)

Cristina, Nomi, Maggie, and I finally got in a game of tennis this afternoon. We started out being really serious, as if we were playing at the Open or something, but eventually that all fell apart and we played like we usually do. Like the Marx brothers. It was hilarious. Nomi said the only thing that could've made it funnier was if Zelda'd come as ball girl (instead of putting the balls in the bucket, she throws them at you). Went over to Cristina's for a swim after that. Mrs. Palacio was going to the mall, so I figured I could get a ride with her and meet Connor so he didn't have to come all the way to my house to pick me up. Then the others decided to come too, naturally. Connor says we're like wolves — we only run in packs. I said we're more like sheep. We don't go far and we stop a lot to eat.

Connor and I sat on the deck and gazed at the stars and kissed and gazed at the stars and kissed and gazed at the stars and talked and talked and then we kissed some more. Now I know what people mean when they say they feel like they're floating on a cloud. Nomi says you can get the same result from meditation. I said but I bet it's not as much fun.

*   *   *

Nomi's having everybody over tomorrow night. We're going to start up the fire pit. It's kind of like camping, only you get to go home and sleep in your own bed. Anyway, Connor can't make it. I told him that it didn't matter because he can meet everybody at Movie Club on Thursday. He said he's an idiot. He forgot about Movie Club. There's a game on Thursday. I said I thought the game was on Wednesday after work. He said it's been changed to Thursday afternoon. Then we're all going for pizza. He kept saying how sorry he was that he hadn't told me. He said, "Do you forgive me, babe?" Babe! I said there was nothing to forgive.

SUNDAY

Mike says she knows it makes her life more exciting, but she can't stand the suspense of not knowing which shift she'll be doing from one week to the next. She likes to be able to plan ahead. So we've swapped days, and now I do Saturdays instead of Thursdays. My mom wasn't exactly overjoyed when I told her. She said, "I thought this was only temporary." I said it was. She said, "And pottery? What about that? You've already paid for the summer." I said I'd figure something out.

Gus wanted to know if it was Ely she saw dressed as a carrot drinking a soda in the diner this afternoon. I said probably.

Went over to Nomi's for the fire pit. And there was Ely. For a second I actually thought ohmygod Nomi was serious about Ely and dumped Jax (and didn't tell me!). But it was Louie who invited him. Apparently they spent the day driving around with Ely dressed as the Vegetable Avenger. I told him my sister saw him in the diner. He said she should've come in and said hello. Louie wanted to know where my boyfriend the invisible man was. I said his name's Connor. Jax said he couldn't believe Conan would pass up the opportunity to eat baked potatoes covered in soot. I said his name's Connor. Grady said but you and Colin are coming on Thursday, right? It's boys' pick, so he doesn't have to worry about staying awake. (All the guys except Louie fell asleep during *Moonstruck*. Maggie tied Grady's laces together, so when he stood up he fell over. It was hilarious.) I said his name's Connor. And then I explained about the game. Louie said, "You see? I don't think this guy exists. Hildy's making him up." I said the truth is that he's a superhero, so there are a lot of claims on his time. Ely objected. He said, "This town isn't big enough for two champions of truth, justice, and the American Way." I said it's OK; he's not a root vegetable.

Connor texted me during lulls in whatever it was he was doing. It didn't take long for everybody to catch on. *"Love Finds Andy Hardy,"* muttered Louie, "no matter where she goes." Nomi groaned as if she just missed the train. "What does he think'll happen if he doesn't hear from you every half hour?" I said well, maybe he misses me. Grady said, "But you haven't gone anywhere." Maggie rolled her eyes at him. She said she figures I found the only boy with a grain of romance in him this side of the Atlantic. Cristina said if I could clone him, I'd make a fortune. But every time I got another message, there were a lot of squeals and sighs and Jax in this high, squeaky voice saying, "Be still, my quivering heart!" Followed by hysterical laughter (even from the romantics). Anyway, the potatoes finally looked like lumps of coal, so we got all involved in eating, and then because there's no way of stopping them, Kruger and Jax got out their guitars (and Sara got out a couple of Mrs. Slevka's pots), so I stopped answering Connor's texts. When I suddenly got a call, I didn't even check to see who it was. I just answered automatically. I figured it was one of my parents and there was some emergency at home. It was Connor. He thought there was some emergency with *me*. Because I wasn't answering his texts. The music was pretty loud, but Louie was louder. "Is it lover boy?" he yelled. Connor wanted to know what that noise was. I said it was nothing. "It is!" Louie screamed. "It's lover boy!" I tried to kick him, but he moved out of my way. I was trying not to talk too loudly, because I didn't want everybody else to stop singing and talking to listen to me. Connor kept saying, "What? What? I can't hear you, Hildy." I said I'd call him back when I got home. He didn't hear me. I said it again. He still didn't hear me. Ely and Louie both shouted, "She'll call you back when she gets home!" My phone went dead. Well, it didn't go dead—he ended the call. I couldn't enjoy myself after that, so I left early. Connor was a little cool when I got him. All monosyllabic and lively as roadkill. Yes. No. OK. You'd think I was his mother, questioning him about how his night was. I asked him what was wrong. He said, "Nothing." I said it didn't feel like nothing. It felt like he was mad at me. He said he wasn't mad, exactly. But that I wasn't straight with him. He hates that. I didn't know what he was talking about. He said I'd told him we were having a fire pit, not a party. I'd never said anything about going to a party. I said that's because I didn't go to a party. We had a fire pit. But, you know, it wasn't the kind where you take a vow of silence. He said maybe I thought I was being funny, but it sounded like a party to him. He heard music. I said you heard Jax and Kruger on guitar and Sara playing a soup pot and two saucepans. It was only a party if you call a bunch of people sitting around a pit with a fire in it talking and singing along to songs that nobody really knows the words to a party. He said I didn't have to be sarcastic. He only called because he was afraid something had happened to me. I said like what? That I fell into the fire? He said things like that happen all the time. I didn't know what to say to that (DO THEY?), so I didn't say anything. (And it is sweet that he cares about me so much. The time I got stuck on the roof and called my dad, he didn't exactly rush home to get me down.) Connor said that was why he was a little annoyed, because I wouldn't even talk to him and he was so worried. I said, "I couldn't hear you. You might as well've been talking through a tin can and a piece of string." He said I could've moved away from the noise. Why didn't I just go up by the house? I felt awful. I felt the way I did the time I accidentally killed my goldfish. How could I be so stupid? Why didn't I think of that? And I *was* being sarcastic. When all he was doing was being concerned. I said

I was really sorry. I didn't mean to upset him. He said he knows that—he knows I'm not like that. But some girls are. Some girls don't think about anybody but themselves. They don't give a false eyelash who they hurt. He said he didn't want to fight with me. Fighting's another thing he hates. And I don't? Do I look like Muhammad Ali? Connor laughed and said, "Nothing like him. You're much thinner." So everything was OK in the end. Phew! I couldn't stand it when I thought he was mad at me. It made me want to get into that hole in the ground and never come out.

MONDAY

I said I'd mind Zelda while my folks went out, so Connor came over to hang with us. When he got here, my dad said, "What? You again?" We watched a movie with Zelda. After she went to bed, we sat on the couch and kissed and cuddled. It was really lovely. We didn't mention last night. I think it's better just to act like it never happened. (Like Gran always says, "If the bear's asleep, don't wake it up.") Which of course is the exact opposite of my parents. They never let anything go. They'd wake up every bear in the woods. I swear, they're still arguing about things that happened before they were born.

Gus came home while Connor was here. She was in a good mood (for a change) and pretended she didn't know who Connor was. "Oh, you must be Aidan — Oh, no, not Aidan, Elwood — Oh, no, not Elwood . . . Don't tell me, don't tell me, it's right on the tip of my tongue . . ." When he didn't exactly fall over laughing, she grabbed his hand and shook it. She said, "Don't look so worried. Of course I know who you are. You're Connor. You go to Priestly-Hamilton, you live out by the lake, and you nearly drowned my sister." She hovered around for a while talking about school and boats and his job and stuff like that. Until she finally noticed that I was willing her to shut up and go away. And she shut up and went.

Connor wanted to know who those boys were. I said what boys? He said, "The ones your sister mentioned." He said he thought I'd said that I'd never had a boyfriend before. I said I haven't. Gus was just kidding. He said, "Oh. Kidding." But he sounded like I'd just told him the moon is made of cheese. *Oh. Cheese.*

*   *   *

Connor's parents invited me to supper tomorrow. I wasn't expecting that. I had to think about it for a second. Connor said, "What? You're already busy?" I said not busy, exactly. But I'd kind of promised Louie I'd help him with his editing tomorrow night. Connor said, "Oh. Right. Your friend Louie." I felt really bad. I mean, what's wrong with me? What are my priorities? I can help Louie anytime. He lives across the road. I said, "It wasn't really a promise. I just said I'd go if I wasn't doing anything else. But now I am."

Connor says he thinks it would be better if I didn't bring all my friends with me when I come to see him at work anymore. He doesn't think his supervisor likes it. She made some crack about seagulls at the beach. I was incredulous. About *us*? He said, "Well, you do make a lot of noise. Especially Maggie. She has that laugh." Which I did think was a little harsh. Maggie's laugh is a lot more like a crane than a seagull. All I can say is it's a good thing we didn't have Zelda with us.

He's definitely a great kisser!

And I'm definitely getting better!!!!

TUESDAY

When I came out to breakfast this morning, Zelda was standing on her head by the back door (she thinks it'll make her hair grow faster), and Gus was finishing her coffee. I asked what she thought of Connor. She said he seemed OK. Not in a peach-silk-shirt way, but OK. And then she said, "He looks kind of familiar. His last name's Bowden, right? Does he have a brother?" I thought I was going to fall over like an axed tree. Would I rather find out I was related to Godzilla than to a girl who dated Calvin Bowden? Yes, I would. I think I shrieked. "Oh, please. Please tell me you didn't go out with Cal!" Gus stuck up her thumbs. "Gotcha!" I thought she was going to gag, she was laughing so much. She came back into the kitchen before she left to get her lunch. I was reading a message on my phone. She wanted to know why Connor texts me all the time. I said because he's my boyfriend. She said that isn't actually the definition of the word *boyfriend*.

Ely asked if everything's cool. I said, "What are we talking about?" He said, "Sunday night. You left the party pretty abruptly after Connor called." I said, "It wasn't a party. It was a fire pit." Ely said, "So? Is everything cool?" I said if everything got any cooler, I'd have frostbite. I said, "And anyway, you're going to see for yourself, 'cause he's picking me up after work." Ely wanted to know if he could take a picture to prove to Louie that Connor really exists. With that scalpel-like wit, it's amazing Ely's never thought of being a comedian. No, it's not just amazing. It's criminal. With all the troubles in the world, people need to be able to laugh, and it might as well be at him. Ely said maybe we could do a double act. And that reminded him about Louie's movie about the Vegetable Avenger. Ely figures it'd be even better if Lethal Lettuce was in it. We could do some street theater. Raise awareness of the plight of the humble potato. Not to mention the struggling organic farmer with multinational food giants messing up his crops and threatening to sue him. I said I thought this was meant to be an advertising gimmick. You know, like Ronald McDonald. Ely said, "But it could be so much more."

Connor and I texted back and forth all day. Green Pickup Guy came by when I was right in the middle of a sentence, so he had to wait a few seconds while I finished. He said it made you wonder what people did before they had cell phones. Ely said, "They talked to the people they were with, not the people they weren't with."

And he gave me a present! Green Pickup Guy, not Ely. He brought me a fan! I said what's this for? He said because yours drowned. He just happened to see it and thought of me. I was really touched. He said to keep it away from my sister.

Connor's parents aren't anything like my parents. To start with, they're very grown-up looking (he looks like a lawyer, which he is, and she looks like Meryl Streep, which she isn't). They act pretty grown-up, too. You wouldn't catch one of them hanging a plastic dinosaur from the kitchen light. I wasn't really nervous till I saw them. And then I was nothing but exposed nerves that were being zapped by electricity. I was in my jeans and a T-shirt from work. I smelled like the herb basket on the stand. I couldn't think of anything to say. Even though it was just a regular night, Mr. Bowden was wearing slacks and a dress shirt with *cuff links* and a tie (but loose), and Mrs. Bowden had on this linen dress and gold jewelry that made her look as if she was going out to dinner at some fancy restaurant. My mother always has bits of yarn stuck to her clothes or her hair and my dad's only tie is a string one with a lizard bolo. (And if he found a cuff link he'd think it was something that fell out of a car.) The only time they dress up is for major celebrations of happiness or grief. (They both own one suit.) But the Bowdens didn't sniff the air and mutter, "Is that basil? Do I smell thyme?" Or ask me if I was going to change for dinner or anything like that. They were super polite and pleasant. But it was kind of like a house that looks really clean because everything's been stuffed in the closet and under the couch. And it didn't take long to see what Connor meant when he said they're critical. Really. The two of them should be reviewing movies or something. He could hardly pick up his fork without one of them telling him he was doing it wrong. It was all *I don't think so, Connor. . . . That can't be true, Connor. . . . Connor, where did you ever hear that?* But by the time they got to the bottom of one of Mr. Bowden's bottles from his wine rack, they'd started in on each other. Not yelling or anything like that. They were really calm and smiling (which is the other way they're not like my parents). Whatever one said, the other corrected. *I beg to differ, Natalie. . . . I'm sorry, Porter, but I don't think that's quite right. . . . Not blue, green. Not Thursday, Monday. Not Nantucket, Martha's Vineyard.* If Mrs. Bowden said she liked to drive, Mr. Bowden would say it was too bad she never learned to park. And then he'd chuckle so we'd all know he was just teasing her. If Mr. Bowden said he liked to cook, Mrs. Bowden would say no wonder, since he only does it once every five years. And then she'd laugh so we'd all know she was teasing *him*. That kind of thing. It was excruciating. No wonder they never argue. They're in a constant state of war. Connor says he tries not to notice. It's like not noticing that bombs are falling all over your yard.

After dinner, Connor and I went down to the lake and walked along the shore. He told me how once when he was little they visited his uncle in Maryland and he and his dad and Cal went out on the uncle's boat at night. The bay was filled with luminous fish. Connor thought the stars were falling from the sky and started to cry. (How completely adorable is *that*?)

Connor says I told him Ely's funny-looking. I said, "No, I said Ely's very tall and he's funny, but I never said he's funny-looking." He said I *definitely* said funny-looking. Since I don't think Ely *is* funny-looking (the Countess says he reminds her of the young Ronald Colman), I really don't think I ever said that, but even if I did, I don't see what it matters. Connor said he hates it when I don't tell him the truth. I said I always tell him the truth. The only time Ely looks funny is when he's playing the ukulele. Or is dressed as a carrot. I said it's too bad he didn't get a chance to talk to him, because he's a really interesting guy. Connor said, "I bet he is."

Mrs. Chimurro at the pottery studio said I could switch over to her Monday-night class for the rest of the summer if I want. Connor couldn't understand why I wanted to change my classes. He said I thought you go on Saturdays. I said I used to go on Saturdays, but that was before I worked on Saturdays. I explained that besides not wanting to lose the money I paid, I have to finish the Masiados' mugs before their anniversary. Which isn't that far away now. Connor wanted to know if I'd started working Saturdays so I could work with Ely more. Because he's so interesting and funny. I said no, Connor. I switched so I'd have Thursdays off with you. Connor said, "Oh." Then he said the game was back on for tomorrow.

WEDNESDAY

I was hoping the other guys would be bringing dates this time when we went out after the game, but no such luck. So it was back to the Big Boot Pizzeria, at the round table in the far corner with the boys—Connor, Stu, Albie, JC, and Milt. They were all as excited as little kids at a party because they'd won again. Which isn't exactly a regular event. Even Stu, who I was surprised knew my name, since last time he'd acted as if I wasn't there at all, said, "Maybe Hildy really is bringing us luck. Maybe we should make her our mascot. We should give her one of our T-shirts to wear." (I didn't mention that to Nomi. You know what she's like. If there's an argument within a five-hundred-mile radius, Nomi will find it. She wouldn't think it was cute, me being their mascot. She'd think it was patronizing. As if I was a dog. She'd want to know why I didn't slap my pizza over his head.) But after that, it was all the same talk about the Game and the other team and our team and some guy who couldn't tell a foul from a bagel, and I started drifting off the way I do when my dad starts explaining how to clean a carburetor. And then Milt, who was sitting on my other side, suddenly started talking to me. He's all bluesed out because his girlfriend dumped him. He said he couldn't really talk to his friends about it, because they didn't like her to begin with. And anyway, you know what guys are like. I almost said no, I don't, only he didn't give me a chance to say anything. So he told me all about Salome Hornstein. She wouldn't even tell him why she was through with him. Or what was wrong with him. Or give him another chance. It was just, *So long, Milton. Don't call me and I won't call you.* He's pretty sure she already has a new boyfriend. He said he felt like a fish that was about to be dinner. I was trying to cheer him up, so I said, "Breaded? Baked? Garnished with parsley and lemon?" He said, "No, gutted."

Connor was quiet on the way home. I figured he was tired from the game. And three extra-large pizzas (after all that chewing, it was no wonder he couldn't work his jaw). He was really concentrating on his driving, like any minute he was expecting a deer to jump out at him. (My mom would've been delirious if she'd seen him. He was like a video for road safety.) Finally when we got to my

114

house, he wanted to know what Milt and I were talking about. We looked like we were plotting the overthrow of the government. I said that we were actually talking about how Salome Hornstein kicked his heart into the gutter of love. Connor said he told Milt right from the start that she was a flirt. He said, "She even flirted with me, and I'm Milt's best friend." Then he opened the glove compartment and took out my fan. I thought I'd lost it, but it must've fallen out of my bag the other night. I was really happy to get it back. Connor wanted to know why Green Pickup Guy gave me a fan. I said because Zelda killed mine. He said that didn't explain why Green Pickup Guy bought me a new one. I said just because he's nice, that's all. Connor said he must be practically a saint to buy stuff for a girl he gets his potatoes from. Then he said he had to go home. His father's laying down the law. I said well, he is a lawyer. Connor said, "Yeah." So there was no steaming up the windows of the car tonight.

Nomi said I should've asked Connor if when Salome Hornstein flirted with him he flirted back. See what I mean about her?

It's really weird. Nothing happened with me and Connor, but I kind of feel like it did. It reminds me of when I went to Nomi's fire pit and he acted like he was mad at me but he said he wasn't. I'm being paranoid. He can't be mad at me. I haven't done anything.

THURSDAY

No *Good morning!* text from Connor. Figured he probably overslept and had to race to work. Texted him while I was having breakfast. Called a couple of times, got the voice mail. Nomi thinks I'm winding myself up over nothing. Welcome to the real world. She said she can go days without hearing from Jax. (As if there's any comparison between her and Jax, and me and Connor.) I said but Connor always texts me. And he usually calls me on his breaks. Nomi said well, maybe he's really busy at work. Or he lost his phone or left it at home or the dog ate it or something. Didn't Louie's dog eat his phone once? (That was Scorsese. Of course. Louie figured Scorsese was having trouble dialing so he ate it in frustration.) I said but what if it's None of the Above? What if something happened to him? What if he had an accident on the way home? You're always reading about youths whose lives are cut tragically short because they skidded in the snow and lost control of the car. Nomi said, "Hildy, it's July. If he skidded on snow, he's some kind of magician, and you don't have to worry about him hurting himself." I said OK, not snow, but he could've hit a moose. Nomi said, "Or he could've left his phone in his shirt pocket and put it in the hamper like Jax did that time." I said but if Connor did have an accident, it probably wouldn't occur to his parents to tell me. Even if his phone wasn't destroyed in the crash and they had my number, why would they think I should be told? I haven't even known him a month. And anyway they're probably keeping vigil at the hospital. You can't expect them to think of calling his friends when they're sitting at his bedside, watching the monitor, *beepbeepbeepbeep*. Nomi wanted to know if I've completely lost my mind. She said it could be the chlorine in the Palacios' pool. Chlorine can definitely do harm. I said I'm sorry but thinking Connor had an accident isn't any weirder than thinking he threw his phone in the wash. Nomi said, "Well, how was he when you saw him last night? Did you guys have a fight?" I said of course we didn't have a fight. We have nothing to fight about. I said he didn't hang out long, but that was because he was wiped out after the game. Nomi said boys are like that. They hit a wall, and it's all over. She's seen Jax so tired that even if every guitar legend, living and dead, pulled up in a bus outside the house, he would still fall asleep.

Planned to go to Movie Club tonight, but I couldn't concentrate on anything but Connor. Still no word from him. Watched a movie about something with Zelda, phone in my shirt pocket next to my heart. No messages. Heart and phone both empty. Called Nomi. She decided it *is* weird that he's not answering. Unless he was suddenly called away by the president to bring peace to the Middle East. She said, "So he didn't skid in the snow, and you did have a fight." I said I don't remember having a fight. Asked her if Jax ever gets mad at her for no reason. She said, "No, he always has a reason." She said she's busy tomorrow, but why don't we go bowling on Saturday? With the Mob. I can't just mope around the house. She'll organize it. I said OK.

What is wrong with me? Am I in love? Or is it the chlorine? I know it can give you fatigue and asthma and hurt your eyes, but I'm not really sure it can melt your brain cells. Although on the other side of Missouri, as Gran would say, they're always discovering that things everybody thought did one thing actually do something else that's not exactly a bonus. Pesticides. Prescription drugs. GM foods. Maybe there's something in chlorine that makes you fall for the first person who comes along. Maybe if it wasn't Connor, I'd be feeling like this about Broccoli Man (oh, what a thought — I swear I scare myself sometimes!). OK, not Broccoli Man. Anyone. Like in that play where the queen of the fairies falls in love with this guy with a donkey's head because she's been put under a spell. I could be fixated on one of Louie's dogs. The Curse of Chlorine strikes again!

FRIDAY

I know that the trusty sidekick of the Vegetable Avenger should be as crisp as a perfect iceberg, vibrant as red oak leaf, and sharp as arugula. But today I was more like a little gem that's been left at the bottom of the refrigerator with the bendy carrots for a month. So it wasn't Lethal

Lettuce who joined the Vegetable Avenger in his tireless quest for botanical justice, it was Listless Lettuce. Listless Lettuce couldn't care less if GM seeds take over the earth or if the rivers have so much toxic waste in them that they burn. I'm not saying I'd lost the will to live, but I definitely misplaced it. I could just about remember how happy I was two days ago, but it was starting to look as if I might never be happy again. The day could only have seemed longer if I was on stilts and being forced to listen over and over to "Frosty the Snowman" played on bells. I kept checking my phone to make sure it was working. I thought: This is what death is like. A phone that never rings. Only if you were dead, you wouldn't care. So it's more like hell. Hell is when you're dead, the phone never rings, and you care a lot. I don't know how I got through the day without salting the string beans with my tears. Really. I don't even remember most of it. People came. People bought. People went. Time crawled along like some small, crippled creature through an ocean of porridge. Ely kept asking me if I was all right, till I finally told him that if he didn't stop, I was going to make soup out of him. The only thing I do remember is that Broccoli Man wouldn't get out of his car because there were too many people at the stand and I refused to go to him like I usually do. I said to Ely, "You're the Vegetable Avenger.

You go." Broccoli Man doesn't really like Ely (it was Ely who told him that first time that we didn't have any broccoli), but I hadn't counted on him liking Ely even less when he's dressed as a carrot. He rolled up his window so quickly that Ely's fronds got caught, so he was sort of bent over with a basket full of vegetables in his hands. And then Broccoli Man started the engine. The Vegetable Avenger let out a scream never before heard from the lips of a superhero. It was Green Pickup Guy who yanked open the passenger door and grabbed the key from the ignition. Ely said it was the first time I almost-smiled in two days. I said it was gas.

When I got home, my mother and Zelda were having an argument. (I know, there must've been another shower of frogs over Lebanon Road this afternoon to mark such an unusual event. We obviously live in a neighborhood where cosmic phenomena are practically an everyday occurrence.) From what I could gather, my mother gave the basket Zelda made at day camp a funny look. I went straight to my room and threw myself on the bed. I figured I'd stay like that till I had to get up and go through another day of doom and despair. And then my phone rang. I could tell right away it was him. I swear I almost choked on my heart. I fell off the bed.

I can't believe it. Really. It's so far away from logic and reality, it's in another dimension. Turns out, Nomi was right. (I guess she has to be sometimes!) Connor and I did have a fight. Kind of. Well, not a fight the way we have fights at Casa D'Angelo. But it was something like a fight. Only I didn't even know about it. (You'd think he would've mentioned it. I mean, what's the point of having a fight with someone if you don't even tell them you're mad?) The fight was over nothing. At least I think it was over nothing. I swear I didn't do anything wrong. Anyway, when I answered the phone, Connor said, "Hildy?" I said last time I looked it was me. Then Connor acted all surprised and said he didn't mean to call me. He said he must've hit my number by mistake. I said, "Well, I've been calling and texting you for two days, and that wasn't a mistake." He said, "Umph." I said, "So what's been going on? Are you mad at me about something?" And he said, "Why would I be mad at you?" I said, "I don't know, but you aren't exactly being friendly." We went back and forth like that a few times. Till finally he said, "You really don't know?" I said, "Would I be asking if I did?" So eventually it all came out. It had really bothered him that I'd spent all the time at Big Boot talking to Milt. I said, "But Milt was talking to me. I hardly said a dozen words. The rest of you were all yakking to each other about baseball. And anyway, he was talking about his ex-girlfriend." Connor said that I'm naïve. He said what I don't know about guys would circle the globe at least three times. And tie a bow. He said that's what guys do to get sympathy and lull you into a false sense of security. I said, "Really? And why would he do that?" He said it's because Milt's after me. I had to stop myself from laughing. I mean, really. I said, "I don't think Milt's after me, Connor." He said I don't know Milt the way he does. I said that's right; Milt's not my best friend. And, just for the record, the last time we went out, the only thing Milt said to me was, "Do you want the chili flakes?" He's just really upset that his girlfriend dumped him like an old shoe with a hole in the toe, and he needed to talk about it with someone who wouldn't rather talk about batting averages. I said and anyway, if one of your friends starts talking to me, what am I supposed to do? Not answer? Question his motives? Oh, I'm sorry, so-and-so, but are you talking to me to be polite because I'm sitting here all by myself while everybody else bleats on about foul balls and blind umpires, or are you talking to me because you think I've been hoping you'd flirt with me in front of my boyfriend? So then we both laughed. And he apologized. He said he guesses I'm right; he was being kind of ridiculous. He doesn't know why he got like that. It's just that he likes me so much and girls in the past haven't been very trustworthy. He'd really be devastated if I turned out to be like them. We talked until my battery got so low I had to hang up.

Then I had to use the landline to call Nomi and tell her I can't go bowling tomorrow night after all. Since Connor and I are back on track. She said she should've known it was like Santa Claus, too good to be true. I said that of course normally I would never break a date I'd made with my friends to go out with a boy, but it is Saturday. Nomi being Nomi, she wanted to know what the incommunicado phase was all about. She said, "Let me get this straight. He took you out with his friends and then he got mad because one of them talked to you?" I said he knows he was being a jerk and he apologized. I figure he has abandonment issues, you know, because he was sent away to live with his grandparents for a while when he was little. Nomi said it's not like his mom ran off to Tasmania with a sea captain. She was sick. And he did go back home. And he was with his grandparents, not in an orphanage. She said he's acting like a mini-monster and I'm defending him. I said besides that, he's been hurt in the past. Nomi said that if he was her boyfriend, he'd be looking forward to being seriously injured in the future. I should've known she wouldn't be swooning with sympathy. Her great-great-grandmother was a suffragette. There's a framed newspaper clipping in the living room of when she was arrested.

SATURDAY

About an hour into my shift this morning, Ely suddenly made this big deal of shaking my hand and practically bowing. Then he presented me with a bunch of scallions. "Hildegard D'Angelo, on behalf of every onion, sprig of parsley, and jar of pickles assembled before you," he boomed, "I want to officially welcome you back to the Eden Farm Vegetable Stand. We missed you." I pointed out that I'd been there every day I was supposed to, just like always. Ely said, "In body only. Either you were looking at your phone or texting on your phone, and if for some reason you weren't doing either of those things, you were staring into space like you were waiting for the mother ship." I said I was sorry; I'd been distracted. He said, "Distracted or disconnected?" And, in case this was something else I was unaware of, he said, I was being about as pleasant as a splinter under a nail. I said I was sorry again. I had stuff on my mind. He said he liked it better when I was a carefree airhead. I whacked him with my scallions. "You forget who you're dealing with," said Ely. "I'm the Vegetable Avenger." He picked up a carrot and started to fence me. We were jumping around the parking lot shouting, *"Touché!"* and *"En garde!"* and laughing when, out of the corner of my eye, I saw this red car pull in. I thought it was Connor because his car's red, and I totally froze. All I could think of was that he might get the wrong idea if he saw me fooling around with Ely. Since I wasn't *en garde* anymore, Ely whacked me so hard with the carrot that it broke. He wanted to know if he turned around was he really going to see the mother ship behind him. But it wasn't the mother ship. Or Connor. It was Blue Eye-Shadow Lady in her old Ford with the PRACTICE RANDOM ACTS OF KINDNESS bumper sticker.

Mr. Bowden let Connor take the sailboat out tonight for a moonlit ride on the lake (on condition that he didn't capsize it). When we got far enough out, we sat leaning together with our arms around each other like we were one person. But with two heads and extra legs and arms.

There were lights all around the lake and in the hills and woods, but if you looked up, all you could see were the endless, silent stars. As if we were the only ones on the planet. As if we were drifting through space. (Which technically we are, but not so's you'd notice.) Connor said it was even better out on the lake than on the deck. (It was way better than me on our deck-construction site and him in the bathroom!) We started talking about someday doing a trip together. Maybe even next summer. We could drive to California. It wouldn't cost that much money if we camped and made our own meals and stuff. Connor said think how cool it would be, just the two of us wandering around, seeing the country. Like that song. I didn't know what song he meant, but I said yes. The painted desert. Sunset over the Gulf of Mexico. The Mississippi. The giant redwoods. The Grand Canyon. Stuff like that. I said it would be better than cool. It'd be magical. It'd be like living a dream. Connor said, "And every night we could lie with our heads sticking out of the tent and count shooting stars. That would really be like we were the only people on the planet." Later he told me more about his old girlfriends and how he always caught them trying to hook up with someone else. It had really cut him up. No wonder he gets so paranoid. Connor figures most girls are flirts. I guess you can't blame him, if that's the only kind of girl he's gone out with. I said I didn't know any girls who are flirts. He said, "Don't you?" He said it like I did. You know, like I'd said I don't have any sisters. *Don't you? Then who are those two girls called D'Angelo who live in your house?* But then a fish jumped nearby and we got distracted and then we started kissing, so I never found out what he meant.

Called Nomi when I got home. They didn't go bowling after all because word was out that Mr. Kitosky was back, so the lanes are a Louie-free zone again. Instead they all hung out at Cristina's. Nomi said everything was normal—they were just sitting around talking and joking—till Mr. Palacio decided to go for a moonlit swim, dove into the pool, and lost his trunks. Nomi said you can imagine how out-of-control hilarious everyone thought that was. She said Jax was laughing so much he nearly fell in himself. After he said a few words that can't be repeated, Mr. Palacio shouted, "I'm warning you, Louis Masiado! If you so much as point a finger at your phone, you'll leave here in a box." Then Mrs. Palacio flapped out and herded them all into the kitchen till Mr. Palacio was safely out of the water and clothed. But nobody wanted to go swimming after that. And who can blame them? Nomi says she kind of feels sorry for the Palacios. They aren't exactly having the best summer. I said I bet they're sorry they ever put in that pool.

Told Nomi what Connor had said about all girls being flirts. She said, "Yeah, and we can't read maps or parallel park either. It makes you wonder why God ever created something so useless and unreliable." (The suffragette gene strikes again.) Then she wanted to know what's wrong with Connor. I said there's nothing wrong with him. He's really sweet and smart and funny. It's just that he's had bad experiences with every girl he went out with before, that's all. It's going to take him a while being with me to realize that not all of us are the same. Nomi wanted to know if I could hear myself. Or had I also gone deaf? *Every* girl he's gone out with's been a flirt? Does he advertise for them? *Teenage boy only interested in girls who are interested in everybody else?* Or maybe there's some store where you can get them. *Cheats R Us.* Nomi said, "Remember the time that Chihuahua bit me? I didn't go around saying all dogs bite after that. I didn't even say all Chihuahuas bite."

My dad's making progress on the deck. Gus says there's a good chance it'll be done in time for her wedding. I said I thought she never wanted to get married. She said by the time he's finished, she'll probably have changed her mind.

SUNDAY

Connor and I were supposed to go to a barbecue at his friend's tonight, but I had such bad cramps that I couldn't leave the house. All I wanted to do was lie on the couch and watch a movie. Mom and Gus both went out, and Louie came over to play chess with my dad, so it was me and Zelda on the couch. We watched one of those animations where famous stars do the voices. At least it took my mind off the pain for a while. Not because it was so good, but because those kinds of movies are so confusing. There you are, watching an aardvark or a toy soldier or whatever saving something (the planet, another toy . . .), but what you're hearing is Angelina Jolie or Mel Gibson, so in your head that's who you're seeing, too. I always lose track of the story because I'm picturing Angelina Jolie digging a tunnel with a tiny teaspoon or Mel Gibson jumping off the dresser using a piece of tissue for a parachute. Anyway, me and Zel were watching that when all of a sudden the doorbell rang. My dad shouted from the kitchen, "If they're selling something, we don't want it, and if they're collecting for something, we already gave!" It was None of the Above. It was Connor. He'd brought me a bunch of flowers because I wasn't feeling well and a box of doughnuts because he said there's nothing that doughnuts can't cure. (How cute is that?) We went into the kitchen to get a vase for the flowers and a plate for the doughnuts. I introduced Connor and Louie. It wasn't exactly one of those made-in-heaven moments like when Watson met Holmes. Louie said, "Hey, there. How's it going?" Connor said, "Hi." My dad wanted to know what kind of doughnuts he brought. I figured Connor would leave after the movie, but he didn't make a move. Zelda was too wired after the doughnuts to go to bed, so we took her outside to look for shooting stars. Eventually that bored her into submission, and I got her to go to her room with one of her talking books. The chess game was still going on in the kitchen, so we went back outside. Connor thinks it's weird that Louie comes over to play chess with my dad. I said it was my dad who taught Louie how to play. They've been doing it since Louie was six. Even though my dad stopped being able to beat him seven years ago. Connor said doesn't Louie have friends his own age who play chess? I said sure, but they don't live across the street. My mom came home. She came out to talk to us for a while. Then she went to bed. Gus came home. She waved at us through the window, but she mimed being ready to crash and didn't come out. I wasn't in too much pain anymore, but I was so tired I could hardly keep my eyes open. Even with Connor's arm around me. Which is really tired. Seriously, I could've fallen asleep on a bus full of squawking chickens that was freewheeling down a mountain. The only reason I'm still awake and writing this is because now I'm too tired to fall asleep. I didn't feel like I could ask him to leave, since he was sweet enough to come over, but I kept yawning and saying things like, "Gee, I guess it's getting pretty late," only Connor never took the hint. Louie came out to say good night. He said, "Nice to meet you, Connor." Connor said, "Yeah. Same here." Then my dad came out. Just so you don't think he's been taking a crash course in diplomacy, my dad looked at Connor and said, "So are you two waiting for the dawn, or what?" Connor said he guessed he'd better go.

MONDAY

Connor texted me first thing to see how I was feeling. I said I was much better. The doughnuts really did the trick. It's amazing what a hit of oil and sugar can do. Maggie and Nomi wanted to know if I wanted to go shopping with them. I almost said yes. I feel like I haven't been seeing very much of them lately. But then I remembered about not showing up at Café Olé! with my friends. So I said I was still paying the price for Eve eating that apple and better stay home. Then Mother D'Angelo noticed me lurking around the house and dumped Zelda (who was having one of her strike days from day camp) on me so she could get some work done. Realized I haven't seen much of Gran lately either and took Zel over there. Gran said, "Long time no see." I said I've been busy. She said she knew all about how busy I was. And with *whom*. And at the rate I'm going, she's going to be dead before I bring Connor over to meet her. I explained how he works at the coffee bar in the mall, so he's not around much. Gran said in her day, a girl wouldn't dream of dating someone her family hadn't met. I said my family had met him. She said, "And what am I, chopped liver?"

After that the three of us sat on the porch and had lemonade and played a game of Scrabble. I'm the only one who'll play with either of them — Zelda because of the crying and throwing things, and Gran because she makes up words. Things like woodmama — any mother animal who lives in a forest; sexycar — sports cars, because that's why middle-aged men buy them; twotongue — politicians. Gran says it isn't cheating; it's being creative, but that the Scrabble Fascists who run the state tournament disqualified her. Forever. If you ask me, Gran's way definitely makes the game more interesting. And of course Zelda's a natural at this kind of thing (today she came up with purrson, meaning cat — which Gran says is genius). I was a little distracted while we were playing, because Connor kept texting me. He wanted to know what I was doing. And where I was. Stuff like that. Gran finally figured out why my phone kept going off. She said she thought he was working. What kind of job does he have that he can spend most of his time sending messages? I said it must be a slow day. Gran said, "That phone buzzes every ten minutes. That's not a slow day; it's one that died in its tracks."

Abbie Zeltig (she's the one who makes the life-size ceramic shoes and bags) offered me a ride home from pottery tonight. She was leaving a little early, but that was cool because I hadn't had any supper and I was starving and I'd done everything that I needed to do. I was fixing myself something to eat when someone started banging on the front door like they were being chased by a pack of lions and really needed to get inside. It was Connor. "You're here." He looked so surprised that I laughed. I said, "I live here." He wanted to know why I wasn't at pottery. I had a knife in one hand and a jar of mustard in the other. "Because I'm here, making a sandwich." He said, "But you told me you were going to be at pottery." I said I was at pottery. He said he'd just come from the studio and nobody there knew who I was. I was still wearing my pottery clothes (clay-covered, glaze-stained overalls and a clay-covered, glaze-stained old shirt of my dad's). I said, "Look at me, Connor. Where do you think I was if I wasn't at the studio? Sky diving?" He couldn't answer that one. I said, "Besides, if nobody knew who I was, that's because it's my first time in that class because I work on Saturdays now. Remember? Did you ask the teacher? The tall woman with red hair in the jumpsuit?

Mrs. Chimurro knows who I am." He didn't see any tall redheads in jumpsuits. I asked why he didn't tell me he was going to pick me up. He said, "Because it was supposed to be a surprise." I said, "Well, if I'd been there, it would've been a surprise." Connor said right, but he was the one who got the surprise, because I wasn't there. It almost sounded as if he was accusing me of something, but I couldn't figure out what. You know, since I hadn't done anything. I said, "I don't understand what you're saying, Connor. Are you really saying that I *wasn't* there at all?" I sure thought I was there. But maybe I imagined it. Maybe I was here all the time. In my grungy old overalls and my sneakers with the holes in the toes. Hoping he'd come by and tell me that I'd never left the house. He said I didn't have to be so sarcastic. That wasn't what he was saying. But he didn't tell me what it was he *was* saying. I didn't push him, though. I mean, what's the point? So he came in and watched me finish making my sandwich. He had some potato chips while I ate, but aside from the *crunchcrunchcrunch* he was pretty quiet, so I told him about my new class and how I'm going to decorate the Masiados' mugs with little Sal and Rose Masiado figures and about Abbie Zeltig's bags and shoes (which are pretty awesome in their way). Then we sat out on the porch for a while making physical contact. Which was super nice. And then he went home.

*   *   *

Nomi doesn't think Connor surprising me at pottery is funny. She thinks he was checking up on me. I think *that's* pretty funny. Why would he be checking up on me? At the pottery studio? What did he expect to find? Me kissing a kiln? Then she put on that voice she has of someone really smart explaining something really simple to someone who is as far from smart as the moon is from Portland. She said, "OK, Hildy, if he wasn't checking up on you, why didn't he tell you he was going to pick you up?" I said, "Um, duh, Nomi. Because he wanted to surprise me." She said that's exactly what she meant. I said it was a sweet gesture. And even she had to admit that you can't surprise someone if you tell them what you're going to do. She said, "OK, but after he went to the studio and you weren't there, why didn't he call you to see where you were?" *Obviously* he knew where I was. I was home. That's why he came over, isn't it? Nomi said that I told her he acted like he hadn't expected me to be there. I said that wasn't what I meant. What I meant was that he wasn't expecting me to be holding a jar of mustard. "Oh, of course. The mustard." Nomi slapped her forehead in her dramatic way. "I forgot about the mustard. It's a miracle he didn't faint on the spot."

TUESDAY

For a change it wasn't one of my sisters screaming her head off that woke me up this morning. What it sounded like was about two million very small reindeer racing over the roof. But it wasn't reindeer, it was rain without the deer. Farmer John said it's about time we had a good soak. Ely said that's what they said when the forty days and forty nights of rain in the Bible started. "Yeah, we could do with a deluge." Farmer John wanted to know if Ely was going on about climate change again. Ely said yes. So it was a pretty quiet day at work, since there weren't exactly tons of people going to the beach. Like, none. But it gave me and Ely a chance to practice our double three-potato cascade. By the time we got tired of that, there were five texts from Connor. It's really weird, but reading them made me feel like I wasn't standing in the rain with my sneakers working more as buckets full of water than shoes, but somewhere warm and dry and really cozy. Probably with a fire and a hot drink.

I was FINALLY going to do some editing with Louie tonight, but it stopped raining and Connor wanted to have a Harbor Lights Night, where we sit on the pier and watch the lights come on across the water. He said he was a little bummed out last night because I wasn't where I'd said I'd be. He wanted to make it up to me. Who could say no? It was a perfect evening, and the harbor was busy. Lots of boats coming in and going out. Couples strolling around. Guys fishing. It was really romantic. Until Connor fell in. He went to get us some ice cream, and I was sitting under the little pavilion thing at the very end of the pier, kind of pretending I was on the bow of a ship sailing into the sunset while I waited for him to come back. Then all of a sudden there was this big splash, and everybody started shouting and running. It wasn't until they hauled him out that I realized who it was. Connor said it was my fault. I couldn't see how it was my fault when all I was doing was just sitting there. I said what am I, psychokinetic? He said maybe I was psycho-something. I asked what that was supposed to mean. He said that it meant the reason he fell off the pier was that he'd turned to see who I was staring at and tripped. He didn't say it like a question, but I could tell that it was one. I said I wasn't staring at anybody, I was just thinking. He said that wasn't what it looked like to him. But I can't help that, can I? What does he want me to do? Go around blindfolded? Wear a bag over my head? What if I suffocated? TEEN DIES SO HER BOYFRIEND DOESN'T THINK SHE'S LOOKING AT FISHER-MEN. How would he feel then? He could be charged with manslaughter. At the very least, after all the newspaper publicity and the TV specials and interviews with my friends and family, he and his folks would have to move. Probably to Alaska. And change their name. His parents wouldn't be too happy about that. He said if I was trying to cheer him up, it wasn't working. Loaned him an old sweatshirt and pants of my dad's so he didn't catch pneu-monia driving home.

Nomi thought it was hilarious that Connor fell in the bay. (A little too hilarious, if you ask me. I did point out that he could've been really hurt. Even if all he hit was a rowboat.) She couldn't figure out how he managed to do it, since it's pretty clear which is the dock and which is the water. I said I guess he wasn't looking where he was going. Decided against mentioning that it was my fault.

WEDNESDAY

Connor called me at work to say he'd dried out and was sorry he did his world-famous impersonation of the Grinch with a bee up his nose last night, but it was a pretty big shock suddenly finding himself in the bay like that. I said you've been falling in water since our first date. You'd think you'd be used to it by now. He thought that was hilarious. I'd already told Nomi I'd hang out with her tonight, but to make up for drowning my ice cream and everything, Connor wanted to take me to this dance down at the boat club at the lake. So I told her I forgot I already had a date. She said I've established a link between dating and senility. Hahaha.

It was really cool at the club. There were colored lights with paper lanterns that looked like boats and a DJ. We had a great time while we were dancing. But then there was a break, and everybody kept coming up to us to say

141

hello. It made me really nervous. You know, because of last night and what Connor said about Louie and what Nomi said about Connor checking up on me at pottery and everything. I didn't want to do anything to upset him. But all these people kept trying to talk to me. Guys and girls. I kept willing them to go away, but they kept coming. It was like I was wearing a sign that said: COME TALK TO ME AND DRIVE MY BOYFRIEND NUTS. I got so stressed I finally escaped to the ladies' room. I locked myself in a stall and I stayed there till I heard the music starting up again. I did that all night long. Connor wanted to know if I was all right. I said it was just a girl thing. When we left the dance, we walked a little along the lake. It makes me uncomfortable when there are other people around, but when it's just us, it's pure bliss. Connor said that even though he has a brother and everything, he's always felt kind of alone. Until now. I said me too.

THURSDAY

Today's game was canceled because it was raining again. Connor said they figured the only sport you could do in this weather was extreme white-water rafting. So I went over to his house and hung out. We fooled around with our Facebook pages. We put a picture of us mugging on our walls. And then I used his computer and he used his phone and we chatted online even though we were sitting next to each other. It was hilarious. Later, we were making bagel pizzas when Connor suddenly asked if we were going to Movie Club tonight. To tell you the truth, I'd kind of put the idea of Movie Club out of my head. Possibly forever. You know, because he seemed about as enthusiastic about it as if I'd suggested walking over hot coals. He said it wasn't him who didn't want to go. He's been waiting to meet all my friends. Unless there was some reason I didn't want to introduce him to them. Was there? Which made it sound like he'd been begging me to go to Movie Club and I wouldn't let him. But all I said was, "Sure. Let's go. They're all dying to meet you, too."

It was a full house. (Something happened to one of their amps, so even Sara and Kruger showed up.) Of course I forgot about all the ridicule and teasing we were going to be in for. *Look who's here! To what do we owe this honor? You know, you look really familiar. Don't tell me this is Mr. Coffee! After all these years!* Even Grady got in on it. He said he really thought I'd made this boyfriend of mine up. Then Louie started to introduce Connor to everybody and pretended he couldn't remember his name. Oh, haha-freaking-ha! It was gruesome. When that form of torture was over, the boys started telling me what I'd been missing, and how last week Scorsese and Hitchcock went nuts when they were watching *An American Werewolf in London,* and complaining because I didn't bring any cookies. I've noticed that when Connor's not happy, he kind of does the human equivalent of a turtle pulling itself into its shell. So I was standing there with this big turtle shell next to me. Really hoping that at last the floor was going to do me a favor and open up and both Connor and I would fall through it. But the girls must've noticed that Connor was about as comfortable

144

as somebody hanging off a bridge by his fingers, because they suddenly all started talking to him. You know, in a normal, friendly way. And then we got out the snacks, and everybody settled down. I figured we were home free. But we weren't even near the front door. It would've been OK if it was Grady, Kruger, or Jax who picked the movie, but of course it wasn't. That would be too easy. The older I get, the more I understand that whoever's in charge of the universe doesn't do "easy." It was Louie's choice. The movie was in black and white and had subtitles. It might as well have been performed by shadow puppets. Connor fell asleep twice. When we were leaving, Louie said to him he should try drinking coffee sometime instead of just selling it. Connor didn't exactly double up laughing. As soon as we got off the Masiados' property, he told me he doesn't think the other guys like him. I said what makes you say that? He said it was because they all acted like they know me so much better than he does. I said well, they do. He said they didn't have to rub it in his face. I said they were just being the way they are. Connor said he hoped I didn't think that was a recommendation for them. Especially Louie. Louie's the worst. He thinks Louie picked that movie on purpose because he knew Connor hates movies with subtitles. And how could he possibly know that? Connor said,

"You're his big buddy. I guess you must've told him." I said that was ridiculous. Louie didn't even know that we were coming tonight. Didn't he see how surprised everybody was? And besides, why would Louie deliberately pick a movie he knew Connor would hate? Connor said it was because Louie likes me. I said of course he likes me; we've been friends since we were teething. We ate dog biscuits together. When I fell in the pond the winter we were ten, it was Louie who jumped in and pulled me out. He's the brother I should've had (instead of the sisters I got). Connor made the same sound the vacuum makes if you suddenly unplug it when it's on. He said he can't believe how naïve I can be. Don't I know anything about guys? Apparently less than I know about the language and customs of Moldavia. I said I know the basics. He said, "I beg to differ." (He actually said that. *I beg to differ.* Just like his father!) Apparently, if I did know anything about guys, I'd know that Louie has a crush on me. It's as plain as the trunk on an elephant. Plainer. Connor said, "Come on, Hildy. You really believe he comes over here to play chess with your *father*?" I said yes, I really believe that. You know, because that's what he's been doing since he was six. I said what I didn't understand was how Connor could know so much about Louie when he's only met him twice and hasn't said more than half a dozen words to him. He said, "It's because I'm a guy, too. We know how we work."

Maybe they really do have a manual.

FRIDAY

I asked Ely, if one of his very best friends was a girl he'd known forever but he secretly had a crush on her, would he spend, say, eleven years playing, say, chess with her father just so he could be around her? Ely said wouldn't it make more sense to play chess with her?

Connor called me on his lunch break to say that the guys had decided not to play baseball tonight because even though it'd stopped raining, the ground was pretty muddy. So they were going to shoot some baskets instead. I asked if he was still picking me up from work. He said he'd been thinking it over and decided it'd be better if I didn't hang out with him and his friends. Not unless there were some other girls along. I had to turn my back on Ely (I could tell from the way his smile looked like it'd been painted on that his big ears were flapping in the breeze even though he was waiting on a customer) and move away from the table. I asked if we were talking about Milt again. He said no. He's totally cool with the Milt thing. And anyway Milt and Salome got back together. Connor just doesn't like the way his friends look at me. I didn't know they looked at me at all. I figured if I passed out at the table, they'd all climb over me when it was time to go. Connor said, "What about that crack Stu made?" I didn't know what he was talking about. He said, "About getting you a T-shirt and making you our mascot." I said, "You mean because it was sexist and patronizing?" He said no, it meant he wanted me to wear something that accentuated my breasts. I would've laughed—if I wanted something to accentuate my breasts, I'd pick balloons—but I could tell from his voice that he was like two hundred percent serious. So I said that was fine by me not to go and told him to have a good time.

Went bowling with Nomi, Sara, Cristina, and Maggie. They all said how excellent it was to hang out with Connor at last. Maggie thought he was sweet. Cristina thought he was nice. Sara said he really seems to like me a lot.

Nomi said she didn't expect him to have such a good sense of humor. I couldn't understand why she'd think that. Didn't I say he's very funny? She said yeah, but she got the impression that he's pretty intense. I said I didn't know where she got that from. She said it must've been from her spirit guide. Her spirit guide talks about Connor all the time. Then they wanted to know if we'd be coming next week. I said I didn't think so. Nomi wanted to know why not. I said oh, you know . . . She said she thought asking questions was supposed to be a way of filling in gaps in your knowledge. I said I had the feeling Connor was a little uncomfortable. Nomi said, "What? He doesn't like the chairs? He could always sit on the floor. Or bring a cushion." I told her if she was half as funny as she thinks she is, we would all've died laughing long ago. I said it wasn't that he'd said anything, but I thought the guys made him uncomfortable. Cristina wanted to know how they did that. She thought they all seemed really friendly. "It's not like they were messing with his head or anything. For them, they were really well behaved." Nomi said that was true. Remember when Jax fell asleep during *Citizen Kane* and they picked up his chair and carried him out to the porch? He had no idea where he was when he woke up. I said yeah, they were well behaved and they were friendly to Connor, but you know how it is when you come into a group of strangers. They kind of made him feel that they know me better than he does. Nomi said that's probably because they do.

I've been thinking a lot about what Connor said about Louie. I was going to mention it to Nomi, Maggie, Sara, and Cristina because they'd know how stratospherically ridiculous it is. I figured we'd all have a big laugh about it. And they'd tell me that Connor is just being insecure. That boys get like that when you first start dating. And then I'd feel four or five hundred percent better and stop worrying. But after the uncomfortable-chairs conversation, I decided against it. I don't want them not to like Connor. I want them to think he's as cool as I do.

Three messages from Connor when I got home and checked my phone. All of them signed *xoxoxoxox*. Texted back. *SRY MSD U xxooxxooxxooxxooxx*. I'd hardly pushed send when he called. He was all sweet and mushy at first. And then he asked why it took me so long to answer. "Don't tell me you forgot to charge your phone overnight again, Hildy." I said no, it was charged, but I had it turned off because they don't allow cells in the bowling alley. You know how in Westerns there's this second of silence and then you hear this sound of a pistol being cocked?

Right away you know there's going to be trouble. I didn't pay any attention then, but now I can see that the second of silence after I mentioned the bowling alley was just like in those Westerns, only without the click of the gun or the jingle of spurs. Connor said, "Bowling alley? You didn't say you were going bowling tonight. When I asked you what you were doing, you said nothing." I said well, when you asked me, it *was* nothing. The bowling was totally last-minute. He wanted to know who went. Once again I figured I was home free. You know, because it was just the girls. I know it might warp him a little if Louie was involved, but he doesn't think Nomi, Maggie, Sara, or Cristina has a crush on me. At first, he acted as if he didn't believe me. "Just you, Nomi, Maggie, Sara, and Cristina? Really? Just the five of you went bowling? How'd you get all your boyfriends to stay home? Lock them in the cellar?" I felt like saying that, since we live in the twenty-first century, we're not only allowed to go places without a chaperone, but even though it's considered a pretty radical step, they started letting unescorted women into the lanes. Next thing you know, we may be given the right to own property or even to vote. It's what I would've said to Louie or Ely if they made some dumb crack like that. But it wasn't what I said to Connor. Since he doesn't really respond well to sarcasm. I said yeah, really, it was me, Nomi, Maggie, Sara, and Cristina. We do a lot of things where it's just us. "Oh, really? You do a lot of things together." It didn't really sound like a question, but it didn't really sound like a statement, either. And, I don't know, it didn't sound like he meant what I meant. I said yeah, you know, like shopping and tennis and yoga and stuff like that. There was more silence, and then he said he couldn't handle this right now and he'd talk to me tomorrow. Call ended.

It's like some weird déjà vu. I feel like I've done something wrong again, but I have no idea what (again). I know not lying is really important to Connor. And I agree. Who wouldn't? Of course it's important. (I'm talking about *real* lies here, not stuff like saying you really like the charm bracelet he bought you for your birthday when what you were hoping for was a Swiss Army knife.) But I wasn't lying. I can't tell him things I don't know, can I? Should I have said I had no plans right at that exact moment, but you never know, something could come up? A debutantes' ball. A marathon. A pigeon shoot. A three-alarm fire. I might even decide just to go for a walk. Without my phone. It has been known to happen. I could've mislaid it. Or Zelda could've drowned it again.

* * *

I guess I'll go to bed and cry for a while.

I was in the bathroom getting into my pajamas when my phone rang. I figured it must be Connor. (You know, because I was pulling my shirt over my head and got kind of stuck and couldn't answer right away.) It was Nomi. She left her wallet in my bag and wanted to know if I was riding my bike to work tomorrow could I drop it off on my way. I said sure. She wanted to know what was wrong. I was going to tell her. Nomi's my best friend. I always tell her everything. No matter how pathetic or humiliating. Like that time on the school trip when I suddenly got my period. And when Gus said I smelled and I didn't want to leave the house for the rest of my life. And all my secrets. BUT. But I pretty much know what Nomi's going to say about most things. And I knew what she'd say about Connor getting all huffy puffy because we went bowling. So I said there wasn't anything wrong; I was just tired. She wanted to know if it had something to do with Connor. I said, really, it's nothing. Nomi said, "What did you do this time?" I knew from her voice exactly what her expression was. It was the one she has when she thinks the milk is sour. See? I knew she'd be like that. I said that really and truly it wasn't any big deal, I was just tired from hurling a twelve-pound ball around all night. She said, "You sure?"

I said as sure as I was of where bears go to the bathroom. Nomi said she wished she could see my face. "Your left eyebrow always twitches when you lie."

SATURDAY

So Connor and I had a big talk tonight. He picked me up from the stand right after work. He pulled up at the curb without even looking over at me. I said good night to Ely, put my bike on the rack, and got into the car. We drove out to Captain's Point, where nobody ever goes unless they want to do something illegal or be really alone. It was so quiet in the car you could've heard a moth breathe. And so tense you could've used the air as a trampoline. When we finally parked, Connor just sat there, staring through the windshield. I couldn't stand the silence, so I made myself say I didn't understand what he was so mad about. (You know, since I hadn't done anything.) Connor said I didn't tell him I was going bowling with Nomi, Maggie, Sara, and Cristina. I said I explained that — we decided at the last minute. He said it drives him crazy, the idea that while he thought I was home with my family, I was out with them doing God knows what. I said, "We were bowling. You know, you have this ball and you roll it down the alley and maybe you knock over some pins?" He said, "Yeah." I felt like we were talking two languages that sounded kind of the same but were really different. You know, like Spanish and Portuguese. I had to ask for a translation. And that's when he said that he can't help it, but he worries when I go out with Nomi, Maggie, Sara, and Cristina. I probably said, "You what?" Nomi, Maggie, Sara, and Cristina? He said, "Especially Nomi." I said you don't want me to go out with my friends? He said it's not that he doesn't want me to go out with them; it's just that he worries what could happen. Like being hit by a satellite? Shot at by escaping bowling-alley robbers? Abducted by aliens? He said, "No, Hildy, that's not what I mean." I had no idea what he was talking about, but I knew he was serious. He looked really serious. You wouldn't think he had an awesome smile; you wouldn't think he could smile at all. But he *couldn't* be serious. It was ridiculous. They've been my friends forever. Especially Nomi. What did he think could happen? So I made another stab at lightening the atmosphere a little. I said I get it; this is because you know that they're really vampires and you're afraid that they might turn on me one night when they're desperate for fresh blood? Connor said, "Kind of." Which made me the only one who was laughing. I asked him what he meant by "kind of." So he told me. Remember when Connor was surprised when I said I didn't know any girls who are flirts? That's because Nomi, Maggie, Sara, and Cristina are all flirts. Infamous flirts. Especially Nomi. Nomi Slevka, math wizard, poet, pumpkin grower extraordinaire, feminist, ex-Christmas angel—and femme fatale. Flabbergasted isn't one of my regular vocabulary words, but I was truly flabbergasted. Big-time. I said my friends aren't flirts. *Especially not Nomi.* He said, "What about the way they were all over me at the mall that time? And the other night at Movie Club?" And he told me that last weekend they stopped by the café, and I wasn't even with them. What did I think that was about? I said maybe they were thirsty. He said every time he sees them it's all *Ooh, Connor this* and *Ooh, Connor that.* I said, "They're being friendly." He gave me this pitying look. As if I was so dumb it was amazing I knew enough to get up in the morning. He said, "Is that what you call it?" I said yes, that is what I call it. They were trying to make him feel comfortable. He said he can tell the difference between flirting and friendly, even if I can't. I said, "But they're my friends. They wouldn't make a play for my guy." He said, "That's what *you* think." I said that I may not be able to tell him who won the World Series in 1967, but I felt pretty confident about this. I pointed out that they all have boyfriends. He wanted to know what difference that was supposed to make. Apparently another thing I don't know is that there are girls who wait till they have a boyfriend before they start running around with lots of guys. I said, "Isn't that like waiting till you've eaten to go out for dinner?" He said no. I said I'm absolutely sure that my friends aren't the kind of girls to cheat on their boyfriends. He said, "Not even Nomi?" I said, "Of course not." He said that wasn't what I told him before. I told him Nomi had her eye on Ely. I felt like I'd swallowed my heart. I did tell him that. Well, not *that,* exactly. But something that probably sounded a lot like that. Something about her saying she thought Ely was cool. He said girls like that only go to bowling alleys and tennis courts and yoga and the mall because they want to pick up guys. I laughed. I had to. I said none of them are that strong. Not even Sara, and she's got serious muscles, because she's a drummer. He didn't say anything; he just glared at me. I said I was sorry for being sarcastic, but I've never seen any of my friends pick up anybody ever. When we go to the mall, they shop. When we go bowling, they bowl. When we play tennis, they lob the ball over the net and run around the court. There's only one male person in our yoga class, and he's a grandfather. And then he said, "You picked me up." I couldn't have been more surprised if he'd suddenly pulled a dead fish out of the glove compartment and smacked me in the face with it. Did I? I really didn't remember that part. "Or maybe you were just being friendly." But I *was* being friendly. I mean I thought he was cute and everything, but I wasn't *flirting*. (Nomi said *he* was flirting, but I figured telling him what Nomi said right then ranked up there with the nuclear bomb for really bad ideas.) Connor said I kept giving him the eye. I said, "But you were looking at me, too." He said, "Because you were looking at *me,* Hildy. I am flesh and blood, you know. Of course I looked back." I felt like I'd opened my front door and walked into somebody else's house. I was speechless. But Connor wasn't. He said that I not only picked him up, I'm always looking at other guys when I'm with him. I said I'm not. He has two eyes and 20/20 vision. He knows what he sees. Everywhere we go. I can't walk down the street without eyeing up every guy who goes by. How many times has he been talking to me and I'm looking at somebody else? None? Hundreds! I said, "I don't care how good your eyesight is; you're not seeing straight. I only look at other guys to make sure I don't walk into them." And what about the other night when we stopped at the Snack Shack before Movie Club? What about then? I kept staring at the table behind him. *That* I did remember. There was a girl at the table that I thought I knew. She was older and heavier and her hair didn't used to be blond but I was pretty sure it was Karel Wyst from the pottery class I used to do in middle school. Connor said he hadn't seen any girls behind him; it was all guys. I said, "No, it wasn't. There were three guys and two girls." He said, "Isn't it funny how you know exactly how many guys there were?" He said for all he knows, I'm just like my sister. I couldn't stop myself. I said, "Zelda?" Still no laugh. He said I'm always saying what a flirt Gus is. I said it's just a family joke. She's not really a flirt. It's just because she looks like she does that guys are always flocking around her. That's why we joke about her. She may be a serial dater, but she's not a flirt. He gave me another pitying look. Pitying and disdainful. He said, "A rose by any other name, Hildy." I said you mean you can call it waste material but it's still poo? He said, "Don't you think it's weird that Gus is in her twenties and doesn't have a steady boyfriend?" I said, "No. She doesn't want to be tied down till she's established her career." He said, "And what's that, modeling?" I said, "No, she's going to be a pediatrician." He thought I was kidding. It all went into overdrive after that. I don't remember most of it. Or maybe I just don't want to. It ended with me practically hyperventilating and both of us crying. (The only time I've ever seen a boy cry was Louie when he was seven and fell out of a tree.) Connor said he was sorry but he can't help it. He thinks about me all the time. I'm so important to him and we have something really special and he'd rather die than lose it. I said I thought we had something special, and I didn't want to lose it either. And then he said, "I know it sounds crazy, but I think I'm—You know—" I didn't know. Having a nervous breakdown? Delusional? Suffering from toxic shock? He was staring at his hands. He said, "I think I must love you or something." Then he said that's why sometimes maybe he gets a little carried away. Because it's so scary. LOVE! Connor Bowden said he loves me! I was so surprised, a gnat could've knocked me over. I never really thought it would ever happen to me. Somebody loves me! How amazing is that? I said I love him, too.

So now it all makes total sense. You know, when he overreacts or gets a little paranoid. Of course he does. It is scary being in love. Especially for someone like Connor. Because of his history with girls. He probably feels like he's sitting on the railroad tracks waiting to be hit by a train.

SUNDAY

Woke up thinking something's different. For a couple of seconds, I couldn't remember what it was. And then I did. Connor said the *L* word. And I said it back. Unless I dreamed it. But I didn't. My dreams are never that good.

Connor called in sick so we could spend the whole day together. Just the two of us. (How romantic is that?) He was going to take me to his secret beach where no one ever goes so we'd have it all to ourselves. Connor said the world of hot and cold beverages (and muffins, croissants, panini, and hand-baked cookies) was just going to have to get on without him today. He said we needed some serious US time. I was about as likely to argue with that as a mouse is likely to jump into the cat's supper dish. I know we have a couple of little problems, but who doesn't? I figure it's only because we're new to each other. Everything has problems at the beginning. It's like when my dad got his new computer at the garage. At first it was totally useless. It was like it hated him and had a special mission to ruin his business. He called it the Terminator. Dad threatened to get an abacus and a fountain pen and throw the computer off the roof. But eventually he calmed down and stopped menacing it, and he figured out how to use it. Now he says he'd rather lose the tow truck than the computer. So I was really cranked up about me and Connor being all alone for the whole day. I couldn't eat breakfast. I couldn't sit still. I kept checking the time in case it decided to suddenly stop. When the doorbell rang, I picked up my beach bag and went running to the door with a big smile on my face. It wasn't Connor. But I was so surprised that it wasn't Connor that I stood there for a few seconds just staring at his T-shirt (BE KIND TO CHICKENS — EAT VEGETABLES) and the old bike that was leaning against the railing behind him, trying to figure out who it was. He wanted to know if I was going to ask him in. And my brain finally resumed normal operations. I said, "Ely. What are you doing here?" He said he was being chased by a flock of zombie pigs controlled by the agricultural lobby who wanted retribution for his tireless work to defend the organic vegetables of the world and was seeking sanctuary. I repeated my question. He said he wanted to talk to me. I said, *"Now?"*

Ely said he'd called me last night, but I never answered my phone or returned his calls. I said I couldn't talk now. I was on my way out. Ely said he only needed a couple of minutes. I said he didn't understand. Connor and I were going to the beach. He was due any minute. Ely said, "And?" Well, what could I say? I couldn't say and Connor wouldn't exactly be thrilled if he found Ely here. Or that it would ruin everything. I said I'd promised I'd be ready to go as soon as he pulled up. We had a big day planned. Ely said, "Five minutes, Hildy. Maybe less." I told him to bring the bike in with him in case somebody stole it. He half smiled. "You're kidding, right? There are four houses on this road." I didn't say anything. He brought the bike in. Ely said he was worried about me; that's why he tried to call me last night. He said the only person he's ever seen as miserable as I was yesterday was Uncle John when Aunt Mimi died. I was most of the negative D words. Distant. Depressed. Distracted. Despondent. Distraught. Dissociable. Dispirited. I said, "What about 'down in the dumps'?" He said, "That, too." He said the only reason he didn't assume that someone close to me had passed on was because he figured someone would've mentioned that. He wanted to know what did happen. I said did he mean on the planet, on that reality TV show everybody watches, or just in Redbank? He said he meant in the tiny, weird but wonderful world known as Hildy D'Angelo. All the while Ely was talking, I had one eye on the living-room window. Which is how I saw Connor's car even before it stopped in front of the house. I said, "I'm really sorry, Ely, but I have to go." I was already leaving. "We'll talk tomorrow," I promised. "I'll stop by the stand. We'll talk then." And then I really ran! Out the door, over Mrs. Claws, down the steps, and into the car. Connor laughed. He said he was glad to see me, too. "Hurry!" I ordered. "Zelda wants to come with us. My mom's holding her back." We pulled away like Bonnie and Clyde making a getaway. Neither of us looked back.

Connor's secret beach is a private one up the coast. He says that whoever owns it is hardly ever there. It doesn't look like they came at all this summer, because the house is still boarded up. We stopped at a deli on the way and got some stuff for lunch. There was a young guy behind the counter, so I let Connor do the ordering and kept my eyes on the salads in the refrigerated case. Connor was really sweet and all boyfriendy, asking if I wanted potato or macaroni salad and if I wanted mustard on my sandwich. We stayed on the beach the whole day. We rubbed sunblock on each other and made a sand castle that we pretended we were going to move into. We went for a couple of swims and took a walk along the shore, looking for shells and bits of driftwood. It was about as romantic as you can get without moonlight and a bunch of guys following you around playing violins. Connor said wasn't it cool to have the beach to ourselves? No one screaming or kids crying and kicking sand on you or anything like that. And the best part was I could wear the two scraps of material I had on without every lame-o and his brother staring at me and drooling. He looked at me like I was one of those pictures with another picture hidden in it. He said, "You wouldn't wear that suit if the beach was full of people, would you?" We were having such a great time. I didn't want another argument. So I said, "No, of course I wouldn't." I lied and said the only time I wore this suit was when it was just us girls at the Palacios' pool. He said, "That's my Hildy!" (How cute is that?) It was almost sunset before we packed up to go. Connor said it was a perfect day. It was. It was totally perfect. And to think Ely could've ruined it!

Lovelovelove . . .

MONDAY

When I checked my phone this morning, there was a message from Connor saying I should go to my FB page. And guess what? He'd changed my status to IN A RELATIONSHIP! (How adorable is that?) I can't believe he remembered my password. He must've been planning this for days. I was so excited I almost brushed my teeth with soap.

Asked my mom if she thinks love is what makes the world go round. She said no, she's pretty sure that's conservation of angular momentum. I said oh, come on, not literally. You know what I mean. She said, "That would be money."

Nomi and Maggie wanted to play tennis, but I said I couldn't because I had to go over to the stand to see Ely about something. Then I texted Ely and said I couldn't make it after all today, but I'd talk to him tomorrow. I figured it was the easiest way of dealing with all of them. I don't like lying to my friends, but I don't need them giving me a hard time, either. I don't think they'd understand about me not wanting to upset Connor. And besides, as much as I don't like lying to them, I like lying to Connor even less. I'd rather spend the rest of my life herding reindeer. Love doesn't lie. I really believe that. It shouldn't have to. But if I played tennis or went to see Ely and Connor asked me what I did today, I'd have to lie, because if I told him the truth he might get mad, and I don't want him to wind himself up over nothing. And that wouldn't be just a tiny, I've-never-worn-my-swimsuit-to-the-beach-when-there-were-people-on-it kind of lie. It'd be a real, treacherous kind of lie. But it wasn't just that. I didn't really feel like seeing any of them today. I just wanted to think about Connor.

Zelda was bored, so in the end I took her over to Gran's to shut her up. Gran wanted to know whatever happened to Nomi Slevka. I said nothing. She still rides her llama everywhere and makes caricatures of celebrities out of pinecones. Gran said, "Not that Nomi Slevka, the one who used to come with you to see me all the time." I said we're both pretty busy this summer. Gran said, "What are you doing? Building a bridge to Europe?" Zelda rearranged the crystals hanging in the sunporch while I helped Gran do some stuff in the house. Gran wanted to know why Connor texts me so much. Can't he leave me alone for ten minutes? I said he texts me because he likes me. Gran said Grandpa Jim liked her, but he only ever called her three times in all the years they were married. The night before he left for Vietnam, the day he got back, and the time he got stuck in the blizzard in Minneapolis with some guy who said he came from Andromeda. I said things are different now. This is the age of communication. Gran said telling somebody you're moving the dresser in your grandmother's guest room isn't communication; it's pointless information. While we were having iced tea and those giant peanut-butter cookies she makes with the chocolate chips in them, I brought up the subject of love in a general, casual way. Is it about the meeting of twin souls or is it chemicals? She passed me the plate. "It's about finding the person who'll give you his last cookie."

Connor picked me up from pottery tonight. But this time I knew he was coming, so I was there. I thought he'd wait in the car for me to come out, but he didn't. He was a little early, so I wasn't even close to being ready to go, but he didn't care. He kissed me hello, and then he stood behind me making small talk while I was finishing up on the wheel. To be one hundred percent and nobody-else-is-ever-going-to-read-this honest, it made it kind of hard to concentrate. It was like having a parrot on your shoulder. One that doesn't poo all over you or bite. But it was still distracting. Especially since he suddenly turned into an Olympic talker. *How do you do that? . . . That's awesome. . . . It's a pretty big class. . . . I'm surprised there aren't so many guys. . . .* But it also made me feel really grown-up. When we got home I lit some candles on the porch, and we sat out there talking and stuff till he said he had to go. It was bliss.

Nomi thinks it's too soon for me and Connor to be in love. (I should've known! She's about as romantic as acne.) She says we hardly know each other. I said love isn't about knowing each other. Not like she means. It's mystical. It's like you've known each other forever. She said no, it's more like you want to know each other forever. Which might be something I want to think about. Since, if we're counting, Connor and I have known each other for four weeks. I said millions of people fall in love in a lot less time than four weeks. They just take one look at each other and that's it. Nomi said then why do people say that love is blind if you can tell with one look that this is the person you want to spend your life with? I said because you're not looking for flaws. You're looking for the special something that makes that person the one for you. Nomi said so what you're saying is that you're totally blind to reality. Because you're looking for some magical sign that only you can see. I said I don't know why I waste my breath on her. Nomi said, not to forget that people get divorced in a lot less time than four weeks, too. There really is no use talking to her. Not about this.

Lovelovelove . . . I feel like I'm a song.

TUESDAY

I was hoping there was a chance Ely would have forgotten that I said I'd talk to him today. (Even though he'd texted back: *make sure you do.*) But hope let me down again. He was on me like a slug on lettuce the second I hit the stand. What was up on Saturday? What had happened to make me act like I'd just lost everyone and everything

I had in the world? And what about Sunday? Why did I run out on him like that? Connor couldn't wait five minutes? What is he, a human time bomb? I said I was really sorry that I got him so worried, but there really wasn't anything wrong. I said I must've acted like that because I was in love. It was the first time I'd said "in love" out loud to anybody but Nomi, and even though Ely was looking like the judge in a murder trial (only standing up and wearing jeans and a T-shirt and really tall, of course) I had to smile. Saying "in love" publicly like that made me feel as if I'd been in a snowstorm, shivering with cold, and suddenly someone wrapped me in about a hundred fleece blankets. I told Ely that love plays havoc with your hormones and your heart. I'm moody and mercurial, high as the moon one minute and down with the fish the next. I can't concentrate. I'm easily distracted. My mind wanders from one thing to another like a bee flitting from flower to flower. I'm either so tired that I'm barely awake, or so awake that a dozen hypnotists couldn't put me to sleep. Ely said and you're calling that being in love? I said yes, I am. Ely said it sounded to him more like the side effects of some prescription drug. I said so anyway that's why I was in mood bizarro on Saturday. He said and what was going on with you on Sunday, then? I said nothing, Ely. I told you; I was going out. I was in a hurry. I wasn't expecting you. Next time you want to stop by for a visit, you should call first. He said he doesn't usually have to make appointments to see his friends.

Connor declared tonight South of the Border Night. We went to that new Mexican restaurant that opened up over in Devon. Mamacita. It was pretty cool. Chili-pepper lights, mariachi music, and these really beautiful hand-painted dishes on the walls. I said I wished my phone still took pictures because I wanted to remember what the dishes looked like (for inspiration—my gran would love some plates like those), but the camera part hasn't worked since the last time Zelda got ahold of it. So Connor let me use his. I went to the bathroom while we were waiting for our desserts. When I got back to the table, Connor was holding my phone. I couldn't help it. I kind of snapped at him. I said what are you doing? He wanted to know what was wrong with me. He said I looked like I'd caught him spitting in my drink. I said I was just surprised to see him with my phone in his hand. Since it had been in my bag. He said he'd thought I had a call. Only I didn't. He said he let me use his phone, so what was wrong with him just picking up mine? Nothing. Obviously. What could be wrong? He said I was acting like I was hiding something. I said it's a phone, not a safe. But he didn't look like he was going to give it back anytime soon. Luckily our Chiapas chocolate cake came just then, so I grabbed it out of his hand and put it away. We sang "La Cucaracha" at the top of our lungs all the way home (we only know the refrain, but we hummed the rest). Connor says when we travel across the States, we definitely have to go down to Mexico.

WEDNESDAY

I don't know about love being blind, but it sure is forgetful. Asher Cockburn from the county crafts council stopped by the stand today to ask if I was planning to sell my pottery at the annual arts-and-crafts fair. It was a quiet morning, so Ely was showing me how to do the multiplex siteswap when I saw this man waving at me as he got out of his car. I thought he looked really familiar, but I couldn't remember why. (Usually when I see him, he's wearing a name tag.) He said he was really glad he spotted me tossing onions in the air. He was worried that I'd stopped doing ceramics, since I never got back to him about taking a table this fall. (Another thing I forgot about.) He said spaces are going fast. I said I hadn't heard from him. He said he'd e-mailed, and posted the notice to everybody on Facebook. I said I guessed I'd been a little distracted lately. I never saw it. Ely walked behind me juggling zucchinis, saying, "Hildy's in love. She hardly notices who she is anymore." I said he'd have to excuse Ely, because he's not one of the millions of people who think life is only worth living if you have love. Ely said, "No, I'm one of the millions of people who think life is only worth living if you have polar bears and whales." I jabbed him with my elbow. And got hit in the head by a squash.

Now that I'm In a Relationship, I don't trust my mom to buy my shampoo and hair gel or anything like that, since she stopped worrying about how she looks the first time baby Zelda dumped a bowl of cereal over her head. So on my way home I stopped off in town to get some stuff I needed. Ran into Richie Deckle by the deodorants and antiperspirants. He's the guy whose end-of-year art project of a naked lizard man with a gun in one hand and a yo-yo in the other caused such a sensation (even though there can't be that many people in the school who don't know what a yo-yo looks like). I said how's your summer? Doing anything interesting? A raccoon threw a bird feeder at him. A goat got stuck on the Greenways' roof. That kind of thing. We left the store together. And there was Connor. It was like opening the front door and instead of tripping over Mrs. Claws, you walk straight into a Tyrannosaurus Rex. And not a really happy Tyrannosaurus Rex. He looked like he'd started to smile and then thought better of it. I introduced him and Richie. Richie said Connor looked familiar. Connor just nodded. Then he said he'd stopped by the stand to give me a ride home, because the Mashers have practice tomorrow and he won't be able to see me. He said *Ely told him* I'd gone into town. It could've been because I wasn't expecting him to suddenly be pawing the ground in front of me like that, but it almost sounded as if *I'd* told him something else. That I wasn't going into town today, no matter what. Richie mumbled something and shuffled off, and I got my bike and Connor put it on the rack on his car. Between town and my house, Connor said five things. (1) So who was that guy? (2 & 3) Um (twice—when I said that guy was in my art class and when I said I just happened to bump into him). (4) I have to get home. (5) I'll call you. Oh, no, I'm wrong. He said six things. When I asked him what was wrong, he said, "Nothing."

175

I said so why are you mad at me? He said why should he be mad at me? So that's seven things.

I guess I should've gone over to Louie's or Nomi's after supper, but I was too bummed out. Watched TV with Zelda and Mrs. Claws and ate a bag of potato chips.

I feel like I'm a weathervane, and the wind keeps changing every minute. North. South. East. West. Flip-flop. Flip-flop. You hear all this stuff about love and how wonderful it is, but I must've missed the part about how it makes you crazy. Not like crazy in love, just plain crazy. Am I crazy? I'm starting to worry that I am. I feel like I'm in a car, but I don't know who's driving. It doesn't seem to be me. Or maybe it's Connor who's crazy. That seems like a real possibility when you think about some of the things he says (not to mention falling off the pier). So I tried to put myself in his head. To think like he does. I started wondering if when he's at work he flirts with other girls. I pictured him pointing to his name tag and saying, *Hi, that's my name. What's yours?* I saw him smile and wink. I heard him say, *You want chocolate or cinnamon?* like he was asking for a date. Then I started wondering if when he says he's with his friends he really is. How do I know that he is? He could be watching shooting stars with somebody else. He could be teaching her how to kiss. How do I know that when he says he's messing around with Albie he isn't messing around with someone named Cynthie Sue? I had to stop. It was really doing my head in. I mean, once you start thinking like that, where does it end? I'm too scared to even try to answer that question.

Asked Dad if he's ever been driven mad by love. He said love has to get in line behind his three daughters, his wife, his cat, his bank, and the internal combustion engine if it wants to make him nuts.

To give myself something to do besides brood, I took a few minutes out from wallowing in misery to check Facebook and my old e-mails. I couldn't find any message from Asher Cockburn about the fall fair anywhere. But there must be some kind of glitch in the system, because some of the people who e-mail me now and then (like my cousin Bill and Andy Fogg, who moved to Canada last year) and a couple of my Facebook friends seem to have vanished into the ether too. I don't have room in my brain to worry about this right now. I have enough problems already.

THURSDAY

I must've been thinking in my sleep, because when I woke up I'd decided that this thing with Connor is ridiculous. Got my cell out from under my pillow and texted Connor and asked if he wanted to talk. He texted back: *NO.*

Why is he mad at me? I didn't do anything. Or maybe he isn't mad at me. Maybe I'm the one who's overreacting and it has nothing to do with Richie Deckle. It could just be a coincidence that Connor stopped being able to speak after he saw me with Richie. Maybe he's just in a bad mood and I'm projecting. Like when you walk into a room and people are laughing and you think it's at you, but really they're laughing because someone made a joke. There could be dozens of reasons why he's so sulky. At least if he was a girl, you could blame it on his period. But maybe boys have monthly mood swings, too. They do have hormones. Only

Connor's mood swings happen more like every few days than every month. Is that normal?

Nomi says the mere fact that I *asked* her if boys have monthly mood swings shows how immense my ignorance about the male section of our species really is. So I'm taking that as a NO.

Ely and I worked out a pretty good juggling routine today with carrots. It kept my mind (and Ely's) off the fact that my phone might as well have been at the bottom of Lake Michigan for all the messages and calls I got today. The only time I dropped a carrot was when I saw a red car. It was like being stabbed in the stomach with an arctic icicle.

Went to Movie Club tonight. Louie wanted to know where Lover Boy was. *Don't you turn into a dachshund or fall asleep for a hundred years if you go anywhere without him?* (You could be forgiven for not knowing he thought he was making a joke.) I said that Connor had practice. Jax wanted to know why he has to practice when he plays all the time. Nomi told him to shut up. The weird thing was that I was hanging out with my friends just like normal, only I couldn't enjoy myself. It was about as much fun as being pelted with rotten fruit. Only drier and not smelly. Whenever I thought of Connor, I sank into a compost heap of despair. But I couldn't stop thinking about him. I had my phone in my pocket on vibrate so I'd know if I had a message. But I didn't feel anything. (Except miserable.) Then I started thinking maybe that didn't mean I didn't have a message. Maybe the message had come through while I was laughing or pushing Hitchcock away from the pretzels, and I missed it. He was waiting for me to answer. Waiting and imagining what I could be doing that was more important than answering my phone. Only I didn't want to pull it out to check in front of everybody and then have them making comments and everything. So halfway through the movie, I said I wasn't feeling so hot and left. No messages.

Gus came home while I was fixing myself a snack. She gave one quick look around the kitchen like she was casing the joint and wanted to know where Connor was. I said I figured he was either with his friends or at home. Then she wanted to know if we'd had a fight. I said of course not. We haven't been surgically joined at the hip, you know. We *do* do things apart. She said pardon me for breathing in your air space. Then she helped herself to a pickle. So I made her a sandwich too and we sat out on the a-deck-so-far to eat them. I asked Gus if she thought she'd ever been in love. She said no. I asked how she thought she'd know if she did fall in love? Does she think it would be instantaneous? Or would it sneak up on you like a tracker sneaking up on a bear? Gus said she figures she'll know she's in love if he slurps his soup and it doesn't annoy her the way it annoys her when other people do it. This conversation was so normal that I decided to go for double or nothing. I asked her about monthly male mood swings. If anybody knows, Gus should. She looked at me like I'd all of a sudden switched languages. She said now what are you talking about, Hildy? I said you know how mercurial guys can be. One minute a big neon smiley face and the next they couldn't be grumpier if they'd crashed their car, knocked out their front teeth, and lost their dog. I was wondering if it was hormones. Gus tilted her head to one side. Was I thinking of anyone in particular? I said no, it's just something I've noticed with my friends. *Your friends?* Her head was still tilted. And her brows were drawn together, so it looked like she had one long eyebrow. She said, "Really?" I said, "Really." She said, "You can't mean Louie." Louie? How did she get Louie into this? I said of course not. And anyway I didn't mean anybody specific; I just meant in general. Gus said, "You can't possibly be talking about Ely." I said for Pete's sake, I'm not talking about anybody special. It was just a general observation. She shrugged and said she'd never noticed.

FRIDAY

I didn't want Ely getting on my case again, so I decided that today I'd act as if my life couldn't get any better if it tried. Big smile. Sparkling personality. Cheerful. Songs being whistled. So here's what I learned for sure and certain: I can cross Great Actor from my list of possible future occupations if I decide not to be a potter. Pretending that I was as happy as a million-dollar lottery winner didn't work. The Countess wanted to know if I had something on my mind. I said I'm *Homo sapiens*. I always have something on my mind. She said, "Don't play games with me, Hildegard. You know what I mean. You have about you the air of an exiled queen living in a studio apartment in Atlanta who longs for her palace and the barking of the dogs going off on a hunt." Besides that, I weighed out her onions and then put them back in the basket on the counter. I admitted I was a little preoccupied. She studied me for a few seconds as if I was a tiara she was thinking of buying. "Is it that boyfriend of yours? Have you had a fight?" Ely was busy unpacking the truck, so I said kind of. Very softly. She wanted to know what the fight was about. I didn't say, *I think he's mad at me because I was talking to Richie Deckle.* I said I didn't know. He just isn't speaking to me. She said so in that case you didn't have a fight. One person can't have a fight by himself. That's what she thinks.

By the end of the morning, I'd moved from the compost heap of despair to the cesspool. *Glugglugglug.* In the afternoon Ely had to do some errands for Farmer John. He must've asked me six times if I was going to be all right by myself. As if I've never manned the stand alone. I said I might have trouble if a barbarian army caught in a time warp suddenly came charging across the potato fields, screaming and waving their scimitars and trampling everything under the hooves of their sweating, wild-eyed horses, but I could probably handle anything involving bagging vegetables and giving change. Ely had been gone about an hour when Connor called! Part of me (the part that listens to Nomi Slevka) thought I shouldn't answer it. Not right away. Let him suffer for at least four seconds. But the other part of me hit accept on the third ring. Connor said, "Hi." Normal. I said, "Hi." Cool. He said he thought he'd better get me before rush hour at the watering hole, or he'd be too tired to push Call, hahaha. No laugh from me. I said we were pretty busy, so I couldn't really talk. He said he was sorry he hadn't been in touch. But, you know . . . I didn't know. He'd been arrested? He'd been on a space shuttle? He was defusing the bomb under a nuclear reactor? I didn't say any of that (of course). I said yeah. He said he really missed me. I pointed out that he was the one who stopped speaking to me. He didn't say anything to that. So I said we needed to talk about this jealousy thing. He said it's not jealousy. He isn't jealous. It's love. It has nothing to do with jealousy. It's all about love. How can I not understand that? I said I guess I do. Then he said he couldn't see me tonight because the Hashers have practice again because it's the county championship coming up, but maybe we could do something tomorrow. I said maybe. He said he'd call me after practice if I was going to be home. Everybody was playing beach volleyball tonight and I'd already said I'd go, but I told Connor I'd be home. My room was starting to reflect the disordered, confused, and unhappy state of my heart (it looked like the garbage after the raccoons got at it), so I figured it was a good opportunity to stay in and clean it while I waited for Connor to call.

I could've cleaned the White House. It's midnight and I'm still waiting. Maybe he got hit in the head by a ball. I can't believe I just wrote that! I thought love's supposed to make you a nicer person, but it doesn't seem to be doing that for me.

The only action my phone's seen tonight was a text from Ely saying he's worried about me again. I texted back that there's nothing to worry about. I hope that I'm right.

SATURDAY

This morning it was my mom shouting my name that woke me up. "Get out here, Hildy. You have company!" I squinted at the clock. Who drops by before seven in the morning? *On a weekend?* My mom was back in bed by the time I got into the hall. I was keeping my eyes half closed in case I could go back to bed, too, but they snapped open when I saw who it was. It was Connor. In case I thought I was seeing things, he was in his work clothes and had his HI, MY NAME IS CONNOR pin on his shirt. He was standing in the living room with a bag of doughnuts in one hand and a bunch of flowers in the other. I probably said something deep and meaningful, like what are you doing here? He right away started apologizing. He knew it was really early and Saturday and he woke my mom up and everything, but he had to see me before he went to work. He totally forgot about calling me last night because he got kind of involved in the game and hanging out with the guys. He said, "You know what it's like." And I had this really nasty thought. I thought, I used to know—when I did things spontaneously with my friends and didn't feel guilty about everything. But I didn't let it get out of my mouth. He held out the doughnuts and the flowers and begged me to say I wasn't mad at him. It really is like I'm two people. The first me (the regular, everyday me) listened to him blahblahing about knowing it was practically dawn and was thinking sarcastic stuff like: *Wow, Connor can tell time.* The second me (the one I am around Connor) listened to him saying how sorry he was, and as soon as he stopped talking, said of course she wasn't mad at him. Of course she understood. We kind of lunged for each other at the same time and got all immersed in makeup kissing. (Which may be even better than regular kissing.) We knocked over a lamp and I banged my knee on the coffee table and Connor went to pull us down on the couch and missed. And the next thing I knew, Zelda was standing over us wearing her pink fairy wings and holding a bright green brachyceratops. She wanted to know what we were doing. We jumped up so fast you'd think a volcano had started to erupt under us. Connor moaned and groaned and made a big deal of the time and how he was going to be late and had to hurry. He gave me a quick kiss, said bye to Zelda, and bolted out of the front door. Where he stepped on Mrs. Claws. Mrs. Claws shrieked like something that wants to suck your soul out of you and throw it into the garbage. Connor screamed like someone who thinks something wants to suck their soul out of them and toss it away, jumped the stairs, and sprinted to his car. Mom came out into the living room looking like she wasn't too thrilled about being woken up twice in one morning. She wanted to know what Connor wanted. I held up the doughnuts. I said he brought us breakfast.

Mr. and Mrs. Bowden had some country-club thing to go to tonight, so we had the house to ourselves. Connor was fully recovered from the morning's trauma. He thinks we should put bells on Zelda and a light on Mrs. Claws. I don't think it'd work. Zelda would just drive everybody totally nuts ringing the bells all the time and Mrs. Claws would turn off the light. Or eat it. Went for a moonlit swim in the lake. (I think I turned a little blue, but it was still way romantic.) After that we went to the Snack Shack. I was really careful not to look at anyone. Found five dollars just outside the entrance because I had my eyes on the ground! After that we went back and sat out on the deck. Connor said that someday he wants to ride down the Mississippi on a raft like Huckleberry Finn. I said you do know that Huckleberry Finn didn't have a personal flotation device; he had a runaway slave, right? Connor said but seriously, don't you think that'd be a great thing to do? To tell the truth, that's not really the first idea I'd connect with the words "great thing to do." I'd connect it with mosquitoes and rapids. But I said yeah. And if Connor was on the raft with me, it'd be immense. Counted six shooting stars! Which is pretty amazing, since we weren't really looking that hard.

Lovelovelovelovelove . . .

SUNDAY

Connor started texting with the summer countdown. After today there are twenty-nine days left of vacation. (*Twenty-nine, we're losing time . . .*) After that we're back on the treadmill of teenage life. I said it's like he's on the platform and I'm on the train, and the train is starting to move very slowly. And very slowly he's getting farther and farther away. And all we can do is wave. He says every day is like a nail in his heart. You wouldn't think a boy from around here would be so romantic. He's like a poet.

Had to miss yoga because I twisted my ankle last night when we were leaving the Snack Shack. Nomi wanted to know if that was because I only have eyes for Connor and wasn't looking where I was going. That's one way of putting it. There were a lot of people around, so I was looking at Connor and I missed a step. He was really upset that I was hurt. You should've seen him. You'd think I'd fallen off the roof. My ankle wasn't that bad, but he carried me on his back all the way to his house. (How sweet is that?) And then he made me soak it and he bandaged it and everything. It's OK, really. And it's much better today. But I didn't want to try standing like a tree on it. Not unless it was a tree that's just been felled.

I was going to spend the day at home, but Nomi, Maggie, and Sara came by after yoga to take me to the beach with them. At first I said no. I don't need a crystal ball to know that beach + girls + swimsuits = recipe for major meltdown if Connor finds out. (If he thinks they're trying to attract guys when they're dressed for bowling, what'll he think when they're not really dressed at all?) I said I could hobble around and everything, but probably I should rest my foot. Nomi said I could rest it on the sand. She reminded me that I've always loved the beach, and here I was on a perfect beach day wanting to sit at home with my foot in a bucket. Sara said it's not like I had to stand up at the beach. I was just going to sit on a blanket. And the salt water would do my foot good. Maggie said for Pete's sake, summer's almost over. There'll be plenty of days to sit in the house when there's five feet of snow on the ground. And let's not forget how much my new swimsuit cost. I should get some use out of it while I can, in case it doesn't fit next year. But it was Nomi (face of an angel, mind of a detective) who had the clinching argument. She got all scrutinous-looking and wanted to know if the fact that I seemed to be avoiding my friends this summer had something to do with Mr. Coffee. I said I didn't know what she was talking about. Exactly when was I supposed to be avoiding my friends? Nomi said all the time. I said she was really exaggerating. I admitted I have been pretty busy with Connor, but a relationship's like a tiny seed. It needs time and attention to make it grow. Nomi said, "Well, you're not busy with Connor today, Hildegard." She was right; I wasn't. I didn't even have to be home early or anything, because Connor had another practice tonight. And because of those two facts, I couldn't come up with a lie fast enough to argue with her. I know Connor worries about me so because he cares about me so much. But I also know that he has nothing to worry about. When you look at it like that, what's the big deal?

So now I know: guilt's the big deal. The minute we hit the beach, I had one of those blinding moments of under-standing. Like Custer when he suddenly realized the other side had a lot more warriors than he'd bargained for. I'd made a *really* big mistake. The beach is all flat and open. Which means you can be seen from every direction. I know, I know. Realistically, what were the chances that Connor would leave work in the middle of a shift and come to the beach looking for me? Not as small as the chances of his parents suddenly texting him to tell him he's adopted, but not huge, either. Only I couldn't shake the feeling that it was possible he'd just show up. That he might. Things like that do happen. Whole books and plays have been written around that kind of idea. And I knew that even if the beach was a lot more crowded than it was — if there were 20,000 people packed on it and they were all under umbrellas or cabanas — the first thing he'd see would be me. Sitting there in my two-piece with my friends in their two-pieces. And he'd know that I lied about not wearing my swimsuit in public. And he'd think that when he isn't around, I sneak out with my friends in my swimsuit to pick up boys. That I'm just like every other girl he's known. And who could blame him? Not me. I felt so guilty that if someone had come up to me and said, "Did you do it?" I'd have said, "Yes." I wouldn't even bother asking, "Do what?" So I refused to take off my T-shirt and shorts. No swimming. No sunbathing. Just me on the blanket with a hat on my head reading a book. They all thought I was nuts. But I didn't care. And I was

OK so long as we were all hanging out and talking like usual. But then Nomi, Sara, and Maggie went for a swim. I watched them fooling around in the water for a while, but then the nervous feeling came back like a criminal to the scene of the crime. Of course, Connor had been texting me when he could, and I'd been answering. *Nt mch bttr. Miss u 2.* But then he said how he felt bad for me cooped up in the house on my day off, and I wondered if he was being sarcastic. You know, in case he really did know where I was. That he has that special surveillance equipment Gran talks about that can tell a person's location from their cell phone. Guilt whacked me again, like a tennis ball going 130 mph. I figured I should check out the parking lot. Just to make sure. If his car wasn't there, then he wasn't either. I took all our valuables with me and limped up to the boardwalk. Heaved an immense sigh of relief. There was no sign of Connor's car. That put me in such a good mood that I decided to get some drinks and snacks for everybody.

There was hardly anyone sitting at the tables, but there were a lot of people getting stuff. I was waiting to pay, maybe halfway to the register, when I saw him outside. Connor was standing with some guys I didn't recognize. He must've come with them. That's why I didn't see his car. I panicked. The thing about panic is that it only involves the let's-get-out-of-here part of the brain. You don't assess the situation. You don't weigh your options. You just move. I moved. I turned around and pushed my way past all the people behind me. Soda sloshed out of the cups on my cardboard tray. Nachos flew to the floor. I was heading for the ladies' room. There was no way he'd be going in there. I didn't make it. Somebody grabbed my shoulder. My life was over. All my dreams of love and romance were dead in the sea of disaster, bloated and foul and floating facedown. I was a terrible person who'd become practically a compulsive liar, and I was being punished for it. Why didn't I stay home? Why didn't I stay on the blanket with a beach towel over my head? Why? Why? Why? Why? Why? All I had to console me, the only crumb of comfort I had, was that I wasn't in a swimsuit. At least there was that. Very, very slowly, I turned around. It wasn't Connor. It was the manager. It said so on his shirt. I started breathing again. And looking past him to see where Connor was. The manager wanted to know where I thought I was going with all that unpaid-for food. The boy I thought was Connor wasn't. He wasn't anything like him. The manager wanted to know if I'd heard him. Where did I think I was going with all that unpaid-for food? I couldn't very well say the bathroom. I said I thought I'd dropped my wallet. Then, because I hadn't dropped my wallet, I had to make a big thing of going through my bag and being surprised when I found it. Then I had to pay for what was left of our drinks and nachos. Which wasn't that much. Nomi, Sara, and Maggie were all like, what is this? Did you get this off somebody's table or something? I said some little kid ran into me as I came out of the snack bar. I said I was lucky to be alive. At least that part was true.

Connor called me as soon as he got home. He wanted to know how my day was. I said oh, you know. Quiet.

It's just as well your nose doesn't really grow when you lie. I probably wouldn't be able to fit in the car by now.

MONDAY

Connor begged me not to go to pottery tonight. He said he knows how much it means to me, but he hopes he means a lot to me, too. (How cute is that?) He wouldn't ask, but what with the championship and the Bowden men's annual Labor Day fishing trip, we're not going to see so much of each other for the rest of the summer. What's he going to do when he can only see me on weekends? It'll be like being in jail (but without the cell and the drab clothes and the bad food). How could I say no? But I didn't want him to hang out here all night in case my mom or Zelda said something about me going to the beach yesterday, so I told him I was yearning for pizza. He said my wish is his command. To kill time and lessen the chance of any of the Big Mouth D'Angelos saying anything to Connor, I dawdled over dinner. It took me ages to decide what I was having. When I finally did make up my mind, and our meals came, if I'd eaten any slower we'd have still been there for lunch tomorrow. By the time we got back, my mom was over at Gran's, my dad was in bed, and Gus and Zelda were building a wooden dinosaur in the living room. Gus joked that every time I go out with Connor, I have an accident. She said at least I'd stopped limping. Connor said he knew I'd be fine if I stayed off my foot for a day. Zelda was concentrating on the dinosaur and oblivious. But Gus glanced over at me. She didn't say anything about the beach, though. All she did was grunt. Connor was looking at me, too. I grabbed his hand and said since it was such a nice night, we should sit in the backyard. Now that we practically have a deck. Blissbliss-bliss. Finally we took a break, and I went to get us a cold drink. When I got back, he had my cell out. Again. I said, "Don't tell me you thought I had another call?" He said no, he was just curious who was in my phone book. You know, because he wants to know everything about me. He said, "We don't have secrets from each other, right?" It sure doesn't look like it, does it? I said, "Of course not." He wanted to know who G is. I said that's my gran. See? It's a landline. Remember I told you she only has a land-line because she's the enemy of technology? And Grady? Who's Grady? I said, "You met Grady at Movie Club. He's going out with Maggie." Connor said, "You *call* him?" I said I might. You know, if there was an emergency and Maggie was with him and her phone had been run over by a car or eaten by a shark or something, I might call Grady to get hold of her. And Mike? I said, "You know, Michelle Sambucca, the girl I swapped shifts with?" I know it sounds dumb, but I was feeling kind of uncomfortable. Even more uncomfortable than I felt in the restaurant that time. I told him to put down my phone and he said, "In a minute; this is interesting." I was beside him, so I saw him hit my sent messages. I said, "Come on, Connor. I want to talk to you, not look at the top of your head." He said OK.

Only he didn't put it down. Then he wanted to know why I was texting Ely. Ely! It's amazing how you can feel guilty when you have nothing to feel guilty about. At least I can. I'm getting immensely good at it. Connor was reading one of my texts. What did I mean I'd talk to him on Tuesday? And that there was nothing to worry about? I said I didn't mean anything. It was just something for work. What? I said the first thing that came into my head. Potatoes. Ely was worried we were going to run out of potatoes. And then I saw Connor go for my in-box. He'd see Ely's texts to me. There was no way "I'm worried about you again" and "make sure you do" sounded like they had much to do with potatoes. I didn't know what to do. I couldn't order him to put my phone down, because then he'd get even more suspicious. I was floundering in another ocean of whys. Why did I ever text anyone? Why didn't I delete all my messages? Why did I even have a dumb phone? So I panicked. Once again. Action, not thought. I made a move as if I was going to hand him his iced tea, but instead I kind of stumbled and spilled it all over him. I don't know what got into me. Really. I've never done anything like that before in my whole life. I kept saying how really sorry I was. And I *was* really sorry. He was soaked. He said he thought I'd killed my phone. I acted as if that was the worst thing that could've happened.

TUESDAY

Ely wanted to know if I'd lost my phone or something. Since it wasn't attached to my hand for a change. I said, "Or something." He said you mean there's been a discouraging word said on the high plains of love? Did you and Mr. Coffee have a fight? He didn't say "another," but I could tell from the way he was straightening out the tomatoes that he was thinking it. So I had to explain how I'd accidentally drowned my phone. Death by iced tea. He said he wished he'd thought of that. He would've done it weeks ago. What a relief it was to have me actually totally present for a change instead of either checking my phone or wandering around in the netherworld of misery and heartbreak unable to find the way out. I whacked him with a bunch of spinach. He whacked me back with a bunch of scallions. It's very lucky that Blue Eye-Shadow Lady pulled in right then, or it could have turned really ugly. But I have to be no-eyes-but-mine-shall-ever-see-this honest here. Even though it's weird not getting any messages from Connor, I was a little relieved myself. Not to be out of touch with him. Just not to have to be looking at my phone all the time. Or to feel that he's watching me. Somehow. And also because now I don't have to delete all the messages that were on my old phone.

So tonight I had to talk to Connor on the landline. Public as a statue in a park. Can you imagine what it must've been like before cell phones were invented? When people only had landlines? And not just that. Gran says when she was a kid, they only had *one* phone for all of them. How did you get any privacy? Gran says she used to take the phone out into the garage. And in the winter she'd have to wear a coat and a hat. Thank God it's summer; that's all I can say. I managed to get the house phone out to the porch, so at least I wasn't right in the middle of everyone. Usually the only person on the porch is Mrs. Claws. Lying in wait. But not tonight. Of course. There was enough traffic for a train station the day before Thanksgiving. First Dad came home. He wanted to know what I was doing. I said I was sitting on the porch. Then Zelda came out to put her dinosaur hat on Mrs. Claws. Then she just stood there staring at me like the Daughter of

Satan. I asked her what she was doing. She said, "Nothing." I said, "So do it somewhere else." Then my dad went out again because he forgot the milk. Then Gus left. She said, "What are you doing sitting on the porch? It's going to rain." I said, "It isn't raining yet." It started to rain. Gus came back. She said people are going to think I'm weird sitting on the porch talking on the phone in the rain. Since the only people who could actually see me were the parents of Louie, I figured I'd take my chances. Two minutes later Mrs. Masiado came over. As soon as she saw me, she started telling me how she hardly sees me anymore and stepped on Mrs. Claws's tail. Mrs. Claws and Mrs. Masiado both did the Evil Spirit from the Curse of the Pharaoh's Tomb scream. It was so loud, Connor dropped his phone. Mrs. Masiado had to sit down for a few minutes to get her breath back. Mrs. Masiado went inside. When she came out again, she left very carefully. Gran came over with a box of homemade preserves and pickles. She said let me guess who you're talking to. Dad came back with a bag full of groceries. Zelda came out and took her dinosaur hat off Mrs. Claws. Scorsese came over three times because he saw me sitting there and was hoping there might be some food involved. Hitchcock came over and sat on my lap. Dad went back out to get the milk.

*   *   *

In the few minutes we actually had to talk, Connor said he really missed me today. He said it's torture not being able to text me or talk to me all day. He feels like he's stranded on a desert island. Only with AC, coffee, and chocolate muffins. He kept thinking something horrible had happened to me. (I never realized what an enormous responsibility love is. It's like being captain of a ship.) He was so worried, he would've left work just to come to the stand to make sure I was all right, but it would've been easier to levitate than get away, because they were so busy. (How sweet is that?) Was I sure that my phone's really gone to electronics heaven? Had I tried it since I got home? I said I'd had a quiet funeral for it. So when was I going to replace it? I said probably not till Sunday, when I can get to the mall. He said he'll be counting the seconds.

After Connor hung up, Nomi checked in. She said it must be killing Connor not to text me every three-and-a-half minutes. I said you really do exaggerate, you know. But I told her how he wanted to go to the stand to make sure I was all right. Nomi wanted to know what's going to happen when school starts and I'm *incomunicada* for most of the day. Is Connor going to turn up in the middle of Language Skills because he hasn't heard from me since breakfast?

WEDNESDAY

Dreamed I was in art class. Richie Deckle was at the table across from me. We were making figures from *papier mâché*. I was just saying to Richie that I thought one of the horns was off on his goat when Connor burst into the room. He shouted, "I knew I'd catch you together!" Woke up feeling guilty.

Connor called my mom to call Ely to tell me that he was going to pick me up from work tonight on the way to his strategy meeting (for baseball—how much strategy can there be?), so not to leave early or anything. Ely wanted to know what the occasion was. "Don't tell me it's your anniversary." I said don't be ridiculous. Our first date was much earlier in the month. He started laughing so much, he caused an avalanche of potatoes. Which, if you ask me, was God stepping in on my side, because by the time we'd picked them all up, he'd forgotten about it.

*　*　*

Green Pickup Guy was buying some corn and we were discussing the best way of roasting it on the grill when Connor pulled in. Connor usually just honks his horn or waves, but this time he got out of the car and came over. I introduced them. Connor said, "Hi." Green Pickup Guy said, "So you're the lucky fella. Nice to meet you." Connor mumbled something about being in a hurry. He was standing there, almost smiling, but it felt like he was tapping his foot and scowling. When we got into his car, he said, "So that's the guy who bought you the fan." I said yeah. He said he thought Green Pickup Guy was old. I said he is old. He has to be at least twenty-five. Connor thinks I should give Green Pickup Guy the fan back. He says it doesn't look right for me to take gifts from other men. I could think of a few answers to that. Green Pickup Guy isn't "other men," he's Green Pickup Guy. For Pete's sake, it's a paper fan, not a diamond. And if you're including yourself in the category of "men," you're stretching the definition, because you're talking like you're ten. But I didn't say any of them. I know he only says stuff like that because he loves me. If he didn't, what would he care how many paper fans guys gave me? So I said I'd give it back.

*　*　*

Connor wouldn't tell me why he'd picked me up till we got to the house. Then he ordered me to put out my hands and close my eyes. I said, "And you'll give me something to make me wise?" He said, "Absolutely." And you know what he gave me? A new phone! He couldn't wait for me to get out to the mall to buy one myself. But it's not just a new phone like I would've bought. One that makes calls and takes messages, that kind of thing. This is a really expensive, state-of-the-art-on-every-galaxy-in-the-universe phone. It's not just smart, it's a genius. It does everything but microwave your supper and dry your hair. Connor was really excited. He kept asking me if I liked it. And I kept hugging him and saying, "Yesyesyes, I love it." He grabbed it out of my hand to show me that besides standing on its head and speaking twenty languages fluently, it takes amazing photos and videos. So now when we're not together, I can take a picture or short film of myself so it'll be just like he's with me. For just a second I imagined the phone watching me wherever I went and calling Connor to tell him what I was doing. Is this what Alexander Graham Bell had in mind when he invented the telephone? Probably not.

Spent most of the night putting what numbers I could into my new phone. Went on Facebook to send messages to my friends on there (well, the ones I actually know, not the friends of friends of friends of friends who met somebody once at a party) and discovered that I have even less than I thought. It's like they really have vanished into the ether.

Got my first texts on my new phone. Connor wanted me to send him a picture, but I was brushing my teeth, so I sent him a photo of the toothpaste. He texted back that he didn't know I squeeze in the middle. He may have to rethink our relationship. (How hilarious is that?)

Put the phone in my bag for the night.

THURSDAY

Connor's working today because he has a game on Saturday, so I went over to Nomi's to get the phone numbers I'm missing from her. Wound up in hammocks in the garden. We were there for hours. We played about a hundred rounds of the IF game. If you could go anywhere in the world at any time . . . If you could meet anybody, past, present or future . . . If you could invite *any* ten people to a party . . . If you were stranded on an island because of a storm . . . We were laughing so much that Mrs. Hallihan next door thought maybe we were being torn apart by terrorist chickens and were shrieking in agony. Usually, no matter what the IF is (dinner, shopping, a train ride through India . . .), Nomi wants to do it with her ancestors. But today Nomi decided that if she was on an old ship crossing the seven seas, she'd want the other passengers to be from different centuries. So she could find out how much grief Mary got for getting pregnant before she was married. And if Columbus was really as bad as everyone says. And if anybody thought it was weird that the guys who wrote that "all men are created equal, that they are endowed by their Creator with certain unalienable Rights, that among these are Life, Liberty, and the pursuit of Happiness" owned slaves and wouldn't let most men and all women vote. Then we got into what a huge language barrier you'd have on this boat between all the different people and cultures. And how difficult it would be to get anybody to do anything together. It was when we were figuring out how long it could take to get someone to pass the salt from one end of the table to the other that Mrs. Hallihan popped out through her back door and thanked God that we were all right. That started us laughing all over again. This is going to sound dumb, but I hadn't realized how much I'd missed Nomi. Tell the truth, I didn't know I'd missed her at all. Since neither of us actually went anywhere. I think maybe she'd missed me, too, because she didn't make any of her normal sarcastic cracks when Connor texted me. Not until he asked me to take a picture. She just watched me as I got out of the hammock and lay down in the grass (he wasn't going to know whose grass it was) to snap myself. Then she watched me get back in the hammock. And then she asked me what I just did. I told her. Nomi said, "Why? He forgot what you look like?"

Went to Movie Club tonight, but I left my new phone at home. (Just in case it can walk or up-periscope like a mini submarine or something.) I haven't been best friends with Nomi Slevka since eighth grade for nothing. If she caught me checking it for messages during the movie or in the intermission, she'd be on me like a cowboy on a horse. And then she'd want to send a picture of all of us in Louie's basement. And how would I explain that? Connor thought I was home packing socks for my mom. Which, in case he sent me any texts, was the reason I wasn't answering. Because we were so busy. So anyway I didn't bring my cell, and nobody teased me about

Connor or anything. Nobody even mentioned Connor. Not one Mr. Coffee or Lover Boy all night. We watched *Bringing up Baby*. Grady and Kruger griped at first because it was in black and white, but it was so funny that they totally forgot about that. And I forgot about Connor. But when I remembered, I felt guilty. So as soon as I got back, I sent him a picture of me holding a box with a pair of socks on my hands like mittens. He sent me one back of him and his team and pizza debris from their post-practice meal. They were all making faces. I said it looked like they were having a good time. He said they were. What about me? I said how good a time can you have packing socks? If I was Pinocchio, my nose would be so long by now I'd be able to smell the roses in Gran's garden without leaving our house.

FRIDAY

The Vegetable Avenger and his trusty sidekick Lethal Lettuce are now a regular feature of Fridays on the beach road. I'd say there were at least a dozen new customers today who wanted to be waited on by vegetables. Only one person was negative. No prizes for guessing who that negative person was. Broccoli Man got out of the car this time but only to tell us he thinks we're cheapening everything Farmer John and the farm stand for. Broccoli Man doesn't like gimmicks. We have a good product, grown in honest soil with honest toil (I swear that's what he said); why can't we just present it simply in all its humble glory? Ely said because it's more fun dressing like a carrot. Broccoli Man said it's gimmicks that are ruining this country. Ely said he thought it was corporate greed. Broccoli Man gave him a that-scale's-off-by-a-fiftieth-of-an-ounce look and asked if that wasn't what he'd just said. After he finally left, I asked Ely what he thinks Broccoli Man does for a living. Ely figures he's probably part of a scouting party from an alien planet. Either that or he does something with computers. I said maybe he *is* a computer. Ely said that's impossible. Computers work on linear logic.

There was one other person who didn't think much of our outfits. Connor came to pick me up tonight because the Crashers have a game in Beaconsfield tomorrow and they're leaving first thing in the morning. I know I told him about the fearless fighters of GM seeds and chemical fertilizers, but he still acted surprised when he saw us. As if we'd turned the stand into an ice rink and all the skaters were stuffed toys. All he said was, "Aren't you two a little old for trick-or-treat?" But I figured from the way his mouth looked like the horizon you see from the middle of an ocean that he didn't approve. When we got to the car, Connor said he wasn't driving around in daylight with me dressed like a lettuce. I said so next time I'll dress as an eggplant. He looked as if he thought that was slightly less funny than water boarding. He wanted to know if I dressed like that every week. I said no. Then he said he didn't know I worked all my shifts with Ely. I said Ely works every shift going. He's Farmer John's nephew, so he's practically chained to the stand. And he's the manager. Farmer John only visits. Connor said, "Oh." He couldn't stay out late because he has to get up earlier than the devil tomorrow. We went to Shep's Diner for burgers. I like the diner because it has high booths. If you're sitting in a booth like that, there's no one you can look at but the person on the other side of the table. We played footsie and had a great time. We were still in the car saying good night when he said he misses me already. (You couldn't get any sweeter if you covered it in sugar.)

Connor wanted to know if I gave back the fan. I said yes. Soon I'll be able to sit on the front porch and tell you if there's a forest fire in California.

SATURDAY

Took pictures all day to send to Connor. One of me eating breakfast. One of me getting on my bike ready to go to work. One of me putting the vegetables out. One of me eating my lunch. One of me bagging up corn. One of that guy who drives around with his pet crow stopping for peaches. One of the crow pooping on the counter. One of Blue Eye-Shadow Lady running away from the crow. And a picture of Ely launching himself at Monsanto just as he was about to pounce on the crow. Ely wanted to know why I was taking so many pictures. I said oh, you know. Ely said he didn't know. I said Connor says it makes him feel like we're together even when we're far apart. Ely said I thought he went to Beaconsfield, not

Afghanistan. Obviously, I didn't send Connor the picture of Ely. Even though it's really funny.

Connor's not the only one bummed out about the summer being almost over. Everybody wants to cram in as much fun-in-the-sun stuff as they can in the next couple of weeks. Tonight the guys wanted to go out to Shadow Point and have a clambake. Only nobody really likes clams, and there's the whole bathroom issue at Shadow Point. Cristina wanted to have a pool party. Only there's the whole issue of Lenora at the Palacios'. Nomi said why not just go to hers and start up the fire pit (clambake minus clams and no siblings). Grady and Kruger objected because they really wanted sand in their food and a major body of polluted water to swim in. Nomi said all right, so let's go to Cristina's. We went to Nomi's. Ely came too and brought a bucket of corn. Compliments of Farmer John. Louie and Ely started nagging me about joining the cast of *Vegetable Avenger: The Movie.* They want to go over to Apple Creek and just hang out while Louie follows us around filming people's reactions. They're convinced it'll be thousands of times better if the Avenger has Lethal Lettuce with him. They wouldn't let up on me. So finally I said I'd do it just to shut them up. I knew Connor would be texting as soon as the team was on its way back home, so I had my phone in my pocket. Had to keep going to the bathroom to check it. Louie wanted to know if I'd discovered the door to Narnia at the back of the shower stall. I said yes. Connor kept texting. *We won. Great game. Going for ribs. What are you doing?* I said I was watching a movie with Zelda. *Waiting for bus. Tired. Miss you. Send me a picture.* The send-me-a-picture gave me a problem. I wasn't at home. If I sent him a picture of me in the Slevkas' bathroom, he'd want to know where I was. I should've told him I was at Gran's. Then I could've taken my picture by the sink and he wouldn't have known the difference. But he'd know the difference between the Slevkas' sink and ours. Theirs is turquoise. I'm getting really used to feeling guilty. And panicky. But that doesn't mean I like it. My palms sweat and my heart thinks it's a horse in the Kentucky Derby. I looked around for something neutral I could stand against so I could take a head shot. Nothing. Nomi's mother doesn't do neutral. The bathroom's all stripes and patterns and wake-up colors that clash with turquoise. I headed into the hall. Mr. and Mrs. Slevka were at their line-dancing class, so I didn't have to worry about suddenly bumping into them. What I did have to worry about was Mrs. Slevka's idea of home decor. This is a woman who's never heard of ivory, cream, or white. Even the refrigerator's pink. And there isn't a bare spot anywhere that's larger than a fist. So she hasn't heard of minimalism, either. When Nomi found me, I was in the hall closet. She said, "What are you doing, Hildy?" I said I was taking a picture.

SUNDAY

The last thing we do in yoga class is *shavasana*. It sounds like something intricate and exotic, but it's just lying on the floor. You're supposed to empty your mind and go into super-deep relaxation. People have been known to fall asleep, but because everybody's eyes are closed, no one notices unless you start snoring so loud that a dozen eyes pop open and Nomi kicks you in the shin. Anyway, I wasn't asleep today, but I couldn't get my mind to empty. Connor was doing a late shift and wanted to meet me first, but I was already on my way to class when he texted, so I said I couldn't. I took a picture of myself holding my mat so he wouldn't feel too left out. So that's what I was thinking about during *shavasana*. That maybe I should've met him. It's day 23. Our time together should be precious to me. If there's one thing I'm learning, it's that love is about compromise. Give and take. It's not just me, me, me. Which is what's so special about it. And why it's supposed to make you a nicer person (though it doesn't always seem to be working that well on me). I was lying there listening to everybody breathing, but I was worried that now Connor thought I didn't care about him as much as I said. As much as he cares about me. Not if I'd rather do standing forward bends than see him. It was really distracting. I kept trying to empty my mind, but guilt kept shoving all these thoughts back in. And then I heard my name. I didn't believe it at first. I thought maybe I was doing better at meditating than usual and put myself in a trance. I heard a few more words that I couldn't make out. I was first in the row nearest the door, and the voice was on the other side. It was a familiar voice but in the wrong place. I couldn't figure out what was happening. Like in a dream when you're walking across the desert and you run into your grandmother selling lemonade out of a truck, and that's when you know you're asleep. Only I wasn't. And then I heard my name again. *Hildy D'Angelo.* It wasn't Gran. It was Connor. I didn't even know he knew where the class was. I opened my eyes and scrambled to my feet. Sunia was right at the front, sitting in lotus position.

She was looking at me. You don't see Sunia scowl much because she's attained inner peace and harmony, but she was scowling then. I mouthed "Emergency" and bolted for the door. I didn't say anything till I got him out on the street. And then I asked him what was wrong. What happened? He wasn't bleeding or anything, but I figured it must be something pretty major. He said he just wanted to see where I was. I said, "What?" I know if I had a picture of me right then, I'd be smiling the way you would if you opened the fridge door and instead of cheese and eggs and cold cuts and a jar of mayonnaise, you were looking at a field of sunflowers. I said but you knew where I was. I told you I was going to yoga. He said yeah, he just wanted to make sure. I said sure of what? He said you know. But I didn't. He said sure you were here. At first I thought he meant safe. In case I'd been suffocated by a plague of locusts on my way over. But that wasn't it. In case I didn't really go to yoga. So I was right. He thought it was weird that I'd rather go to class than see him. By the time we got it all straightened out, everybody was leaving and Connor had to get to work. Nomi wanted to know what that was all about. I said oh, you know. Nomi said tell me. I said he wanted to surprise me by being here when I came out. Just because a person smiles doesn't mean she's happy. "He's full of surprises, isn't he?" said Nomi. I was supposed to go home with her, but I could tell from the way she was swinging her mat back and forth that she was going to want to have a talk about how full of surprises Connor is. She always wants to know "why." Why this? Why that? How come? But-butbutbutbut. She's driven more than one teacher crazy with that stuff. She nearly had Mrs. Stepney in tears once over Manifest Destiny. So I said I'd forgotten all about it, but I couldn't go with her after all, because I had to go somewhere with my folks. Nomi wanted to know where. I said it was Aunt Lonnie's birthday. I half expected her to ask me how old Aunt Lonnie is today, but what she asked was how I could forget something like that. I said because I'm very self-involved.

Somewhere on the beautiful island of Maui, people are looking up and wondering where that enormous nose came from.

I told my mom I was pretty amazed that she had written down the address for the new yoga studio. She's not usually that organized. She said she was happy not to disappoint me — she *isn't* that organized. She has no idea where it is. I said then how could you tell Connor where it is? She said she didn't. I said well, who did? She said do I look like a mind reader? Hardly. She had on rubber gloves and one of those face masks she bought last time there was a flu scare. She looked like a woman who was cleaning the oven.

More practice tonight for the Thrashers. Everybody in the Mob went over to Grady's for a barbecue (safer than Maggie's), but I couldn't go because I was at Aunt Lonnie's celebrating her birthday three months early. Started to make a list of what stuff to put into the fall arts-and-crafts fair, but I've hardly made anything all summer. Haven't even finished the Masiados' mugs. Listened to the CD Connor made me instead till my dad banged on my door wanting to know how many more times I was going to play it. He said you do have headphones, you know.

Connor called when he got home. He said he really misses me. He can't wait till tomorrow. I said tomorrow? He said yeah. He thinks we're due a special Moonlit Boat Ride Night. I was thinking I was due a Making Things out of Clay Night. But tomorrow is day 22. "Twenty-two and I'm feeling blue," said Connor. I said I can't wait, either.

MONDAY

Spent the day over at Gran's. She worked in her garden while I mowed the lawn. When I was done, there were three texts from Connor. He wanted a picture of me with the mower. Gran wanted to know why. Hasn't he ever seen a lawn mower, or doesn't he believe that I'm cutting her grass? I said of course he believes me. It makes him feel like we're together if I send him a picture. Gran said but you're not together. He's at the mall and you're with me. I said anybody would think she's never been in love. She said she was starting to think that she hasn't. She didn't see Grandpa Jim for two years after he went to Vietnam, and she didn't forget what he looked like for even half a second. I said that that was a long time ago. You didn't even have PCs then. Now we have the technology to always be in touch, and Connor thinks we should use it. Gran said it's like using a bomb to kill a mosquito. And then you know what she did? She took my phone away! (She's really quick for an old lady.) She said she'd had enough of my age-of-communication nonsense. We were going to have iced tea and cookies and talk like people used to do in the ancient time when everybody had a few friends they saw regularly and not three hundred that they never see. (If you ask me, she knows more about Facebook than she lets on.) "We're going to look at each other and give each other all our attention. I'm not stopping in the middle of every other sentence while you text your boyfriend." So we had our tea and talked, and she told me some really funny stories about my dad that I hadn't heard before, and then she got out some of her photo albums. We were looking at them when the bell rang. I figured it must be one of her neighbors, but when she opened the door, I heard her say, "Don't tell me. Let me guess. You must be Connor." You could've knocked me over with a leaf of lettuce! Connor said he got off earlier than usual, so he thought he'd pick me up at my grandmother's instead of waiting for me to go home. He would've told me, but I wasn't answering my phone. Usually that would make him all grunty and grumpy, but instead he was in a totally good mood. Really charming and sweet. We hung out with Gran for a while, and then we went out to the lake. We stopped at the deli for some picnic stuff. I could see at least five guys inside, so I told

Connor I was wiped out from giving Gran's grass a crew cut and I made him go alone while I sort of slumped down in my seat and closed my eyes. I figured that was safer than going with him. I didn't want to ruin the evening because my eyes were wandering. And it was the right thing to do, because we had a perfect night. So we didn't get too depressed about how the summer's almost over, we started planning stuff for the fall and winter. His school always has a hayride in September. And there's the Halloween dance. And the Christmas dance. And ice skating. And sledding. And his dad has a Ski Doo. Connor says even though we'll mainly only see each other on weekends, we can still talk every night. And text. And send pictures. He figures it was really fate, not iced tea, that drowned my old phone. I said and was it fate or my mom who told you where my grandmother lives? He said neither. He always knows where I am. His heart tells him. (How romantic is that?)

Lovelovelovelovelove . . .

TUESDAY

My mom wanted to know why I wasn't considerate enough to tell Gran that Connor was coming to her house. I said because I didn't know. She said well, you could at least've told her you gave him her address. So if he showed up when I wasn't there, she didn't think he was a burglar or a con man. I said that I didn't give it to him. She said, "Oh."

I had a really good day yesterday and a really terrific night last night, but I should've known somebody would ruin it for me. Meet Ely Weimer, the human equivalent of a hurricane wiping out the Thanksgiving Day Parade. Everything was OK in the morning. We were Superman-during-a-crime-wave busy. It was as if everybody around here woke up with one thought in their minds: Go to the Eden Farm Stand and buy corn (and pick up some tomatoes while you're there). Which meant that Ely's and my conversation was pretty limited. *Could you pass me some bags? I'll get the lettuce. We're going to need more parsley. That was my foot.* But there was a lull in the afternoon. And that's when Ely suddenly asked me why Connor doesn't like him. This diary will go to my grave with me, so I'm going to be totally honest. As soon as he said it, I knew it was true. But I didn't want it to be. I want Connor to like my friends. And I want them to like him. So I asked Ely what made him say that. Ely said it's something in the way Connor turns to stone and doesn't speak when he's around him. And those looks. Like everything on the stand is moldering rotten. I told Ely he's imagining things. He's only seen Connor a couple of times, and we're usually in a hurry. And Connor's not an extrovert who can run around dressed as a root vegetable. He's shy. Ely said he works in retail; how shy can he be? I said it's different when you have a script. You know: tea, coffee, cinnamon, chocolate? Ely said he's not taking it personally. He gets the impression that Connor doesn't like any of my friends. Ely couldn't know how Connor feels about Nomi, Maggie, Cristina, and Sara. He couldn't. So I said like who, exactly? Ely said he doesn't like Louie. I laughed. Oh, please . . . Who told you that? He said Louie. Louie told Ely that Connor treats him like he's contagious. I said that's Louie's warped and overactive imagination.

Louie's only met him a couple of times too. Ely said plus Louie says he never sees me anymore and he knows that's because of Connor. I said that's not true. That he never sees me. I mean, duh! He lives across the street. I see him all the time. I saw him just this morning getting Scorsese out of a tree. And I've been to Movie Club, and we had a fire pit the other night. Good grief. I could only see him more if he lived with me. Ely wanted to know if I know that my left eyebrow twitches when I lie.

I told Connor that Ely doesn't think he likes him. Just to see what he'd say. Connor said he doesn't like Ely. So I asked him what that was based on, since he doesn't exactly know Ely. Connor said he knows enough. I said are we talking about the carrot? Because I know he doesn't like the carrot. He said the carrot costume did make him think Ely's a loser or at least a serious geek, but mainly it's because he can't get all excited about my old boyfriends. Except in a negative way. Maybe I think that's immature, but that's how he feels. It's like a hot knife in his heart every time he sees me with Ely. I was so surprised that if a dust mite had bumped into me, I would've collapsed in a heap. I reminded Connor that I don't have any old boyfriends. I've never even had a young one until now. Why would he think that Ely and I had gone out together?

Connor gave me this look. If I'd been a scab, he would've picked me. He said, "Because that's what you said." I did? When did I say that? Maybe Connor's going to be a lawyer like his father, because he sure as sunrise looked as if he was cross-examining a defendant. *But didn't you say in your statement that on the night in question, you never left your house . . . ?* Connor said, "You told me Ely's interesting." And that's me saying Ely was an ex-boyfriend? I am also on record as saying that my grandmother, Mrs. Gorrie in the gift store, and Sunia Kreple are interesting people. Did he think I'd been dating them, too? Connor said not to be ridiculous. If a girl says a boy is interesting, it obviously means something. I said that's true. It means he's interesting. And Ely is. He's smart and funny and he knows a lot about growing cycles. Connor sees how Ely and I are together. I said yeah, the basis for a salad. Connor said he didn't want to fight about it. It's day 21. (*It's almost done. . . .*) So as long as I swear it's over between me and Ely, he's willing to put it behind us. But he doesn't have to like him. I didn't have the strength to bring up Louie.

WEDNESDAY

I don't remember any bad dreams, but I woke up in a pensive mood. It makes me really sad that I cause Connor so much suffering. I don't mean to. I want to make him happy. But it doesn't look like I know how. I guess I never realized how much there is to learn about guys. They really should come with a manual. Like a computer. *Boyfriends for Beginners. Dating for Dummies.* Or they should share the one they all use. I feel like I'm on a learning curve that's steeper than the Andes. Relationships are about a million times trickier than I thought. I guess I always figured you met somebody, and you liked him and he liked you, and you thought he was cute and he thought you were cute, and the same things made you laugh or you shared a passion for skeet shooting, stuff like that, and so you got together. Of course you'd have arguments and differences. I haven't spent my life with Vinny and Luisa, the Dueling D'Angelos, not to know that. You're not always going to see eye-to-eye with *anybody*. Even twins must disagree sometimes. Never mind people from different homes and sexes. You expect that. But nobody warned me about how much misunderstanding and hurt there can be. Just incidentally. Because you're breathing or tend to keep your eyes open when you're awake. Don't other people have these problems, or are they just not talking about them? My gran says that when she was a kid, no one ever talked about sex. There was a big conspiracy of silence. She even remembers when she was little being told that the stork brings babies. The stork! A bird? A bird brings human babies? How is that supposed to work? Gran says people thought that if you didn't know anything about sex, you wouldn't do it. Is it something like that with relationships? That people don't talk about how hard they are because they think that if you knew the truth, you would never want to have one? But maybe it all depends on how much you love each other. Like Nomi and Jax. They like each other, but I don't think they're in love. I mean, a lot of Nomi's friends are boys, but I've never seen Jax act like if she laughed with Louie or punched Grady, somebody was hacking at his heart with a meat cleaver. But Connor and I are in love. He said that if anything happened to me, he wouldn't want to go on living. I don't want to make him suffer or anything, but that's pretty romantic, isn't it? We must really be in love.

The Countess stopped by the stand today. She said seeing me dancing on the silver clouds of love reminded her of her youth. (I didn't say it seemed more like the rusty trampoline of love to me right now.) She had her wedding photos to show me in this big old album with wedding bells on the cover (in silver, like the clouds). She mentions her husband a lot (his name was Larry, and he sold carpets), but I'd never seen a picture of him before. Larry was kind of geeky-looking, even in his tux (the short, skinny, glasses type who you guess is good at math but who probably isn't). But the Countess—who now looks like a regular old lady except for the plum-colored hair and the occasional tiara—was genuine drop-in-your-tracks gorgeous. Like Gus. Even Ely said so. He said she must've bruised a few hearts. The Countess said, "Yes, I had my admirers." Men used to follow her down the street. She had songs and poems written about her and posed for two famous artists. I said Larry must've had a hard time with that. She said he wasn't the one who had to stand for hours in a cold studio wearing only a slip. I said no, I meant he must've been jealous with all those other guys after her. She said no. She said, "We loved each other the way a bird loves the sky. What did he have to be jealous about?"

The Slashers have another game tomorrow, so Connor took me to the Firemen's Fair over in Little Hollow tonight. He called it Just Like When We Were Little Night! And it was! I haven't been to a fair like that since I was twelve and was sick on the roller coaster. We had hot dogs and corn on the cob. We tossed coins and picked numbers and threw hoops, and I walked into a tent cable and spilled my lemonade on someone. (Connor says I'm the most accident-prone girl he's ever known. I nearly said I didn't use to be.) We had a bad moment when he wanted to borrow my phone to take our picture because his battery was really low. Naturally, I didn't have my cell with me. I know it's silly and mean, but I really don't like him checking my contacts and texts and stuff, so it's easier just not to bring it when I'm with him. I said I forgot it. He said, "Again?" He said I'm always forgetting my phone. Somehow he didn't make it sound like that was because I have the memory of a goldfish. He made it sound like there was some deep, dark reason for it. I said it's only that I don't need it when I'm with you. He said are you sure that's why? You sure it's not because you're afraid of who might call you? I said you mean my mother? That made him laugh. Crisis averted. (Even if I'm not really sure what the crisis would have been about.) And then Connor actually won something playing darts. He said if you could call it winning. It's this doll that looks like it would kill all your other dolls if you left her alone with them. We couldn't stop laughing about her. We went on all the cool, scary rides and held on to each other and screamed. It was immense! We left the doll on the Cyclone. All the way home Connor kept teasing me that the doll was following us. I don't think I've ever had more fun. It was much better than when we were little.

THURSDAY

Nomi asked me to go shopping for school stuff with her today. Mainly I said yes because I wanted to get something for the Masiados for their anniversary, since I never finished the mugs (they can be their Christmas present). But even though I knew Connor was over in Farley playing ball, it made me jiggy being in the mall. I was worried I might run into somebody who knows him. Just because I haven't met most of his friends doesn't mean they wouldn't recognize me from his Facebook page. He has tons of pictures of me and us on it. I kept waiting for someone to suddenly loom in front of me saying, "Aren't you Connor Bowden's girlfriend?" I couldn't say no if they did. In case he found out. And I couldn't very well ask whoever it was not to tell him they saw me. How weird would that sound? Especially with Nomi next to me. It's not the kind of thing she'd be likely to ignore. So I was a little preoccupied. If I thought I saw someone looking over at me, I'd step behind Nomi. "Good grief, Hildegard!" she'd snap. "I can feel your hot breath on my neck." Or she'd say that I'd stepped on her heel. Or that I was going to knock her over. When I saw a girl coming toward me smiling like she was going to say, *Aren't you Hildy D'Angelo? I'm a friend of Connor's!* I ducked into a changing room. It took about two seconds before Nomi was shouting, "Hildy! Hildy!" loud enough to call the hogs. "I'm here," I hissed. She stuck her head around the corner of the entrance. "Now what are you doing? You don't even have anything to try on!" And then (naturally) I saw Mrs. Bowden! I mean, who else? I don't know why she wasn't at work. Like she should've been. She was talking to a saleswoman. The saleswoman was nodding. And then she raised her hand

and pointed at Nomi. Not really at Nomi—in Nomi's direction. Panic jumped me like a monkey. (Yes, again. Guilt and panic, my new good buddies.) There wasn't much I could do short of being beamed up or throwing myself on the floor. So I stuck my head in a rack of raincoats. I don't know how long I stayed like that, but eventually Nomi's face appeared on the other side. She wanted to know if there was any point in asking what I was doing. I said I was looking at something. She said if the something I was looking at had anything to do with the blond woman who looked a little like Meryl Streep, she was gone. I said of course it didn't and stepped back. Then Nomi wanted to know what was wrong with me. I said, "Nothing." She said I was skitterier than a cat on the Fourth of July. I said I didn't know what she meant. She said that she meant I was acting like I expected a hundred firecrackers to go off any minute. I said she was imagining things. I was as calm as a tree. She said oh, really? Was she imagining that I just tried to hide in a bunch of trench coats? And was she imagining me running into the changing room? Ducking behind her? Breathing down her neck? I said she was misinterpreting. She said and anyway, she didn't just mean now. Was she imagining what happened at the beach? Was she imagining that she found me taking a picture of myself in her hall closet the other night? How did she misinterpret that? I groaned so loudly a couple of people looked over at us. But really. How many times do I have to explain about the pictures? "Because he wants to feel like he's with you?" She made it sound really dumb, like I'd said I think the world's flat and made out of pancake batter. How was a picture of me leaning against a box of Christmas decorations going to make him feel like he was with me? He wasn't with me. He couldn't have squeezed into the closet beside me even if he was. He would've been knocked out cold by an avalanche of old hats and boots if he'd tried. I said I would never expect her to understand. Maybe it's because of her feminist genes, but she really has about as much romance in her as a can of creamed corn. I said whereas Connor pretty much has the soul of a poet. And then I made the mistake of telling her how he just showed up at my gran's on Monday because he was worried about me. She said and you think that's romantic? I said well, what do you think it is? Nomi said, "Creepy. It's like he's a private detective, not a boyfriend." She said she's amazed he hasn't thought of having me electronically tagged. Then he'd know where I was every minute of the day. Nomi said, "Or maybe that's going to be your back-to-school present." I said I don't think she really gets love. Not love like Connor feels. She looked like I was trying to sell her squash. To show you just how weird people are, even me, I had a second when I almost wished he'd drop it.

Didn't dress as Lethal Lettuce today because tonight was Moonlit Walk on the Lake Shore and then crab cakes at the Snack Shack (it'll be closing next weekend till the spring, and it is OUR place), and Connor was picking me up from work. He doesn't like me in leaves. Ely wanted to know why I wasn't in costume. I said there was a major meltdown at Casa D'Angelo this morning, and I totally forgot. Nose nudging toward Australia. But then Ely said but we're still doing the filming on Sunday, right? *This* Sunday? *That* I really had forgotten. Anyway, because I was taken by surprise, and because I felt guilty that I was already lying, I said of course. I'm praying hard for rain. Connor said he was glad to see I'd stopped wearing that stupid costume. I said me too. Nose edging toward western tip of Indonesia.

The moonlit walk was awesome. Romantic. Magical. We saw bats. And heard an owl. And kept stopping to kiss. Connor stumbled a couple of times because it was pretty dark and it isn't like there's a sidewalk, but since I'm used to not being able to see where I'm going, I did OK. There were a few minutes of terror and anxiety when we a bottle of water from the Fountain of Youth. N

"So explain it to me." I said true love is all-co

Connor wants to be with me and to know what

and thinking every minute of the day. I'm alwa

mind. And when we're not together, he worr

what's happening to me and what could happ

and what I'm doing or what I could be doing. 7

he needs to be reassured all the time. Nomi s

body was confusing love with a fascist dictator

FRIDAY

Day 18! Connor says he feels like time ha

jet. He must've texted me two dozen times

because he could. Once we're back in scho

couple first thing in the morning and mayl

at lunch and then that'll be it till the end

because once more we'll be the prisoners of 1

rules. Ely's given up making snide comments

take my phone when I left it on the counte

someone and started juggling it with a coupl

thought we saw a bear. Rustling leaves. Large dark shape in the water. (Connor pushed me behind him! How cool is that? I wonder if Jax would do that for Nomi?) Only it turned out to be a St. Bernard named Arnold. And to continue our perfect evening, the Snack Shack wasn't too crowded tonight. And everybody was a couple! It was bliss.

SATURDAY

Tonight we had our first double date! It was with Albie and the girl he's started seeing whose name is Genie (yes, that's really how she spells it). It made me feel really grown-up, double-dating. Especially since this was only Albie and Genie's third date, so Connor and I were like an old married couple, practically. I knew he'd get extra pepperoni on his pizza. He knew I'd want a slice of lemon in my cola. We had stories of stuff we'd done together to tell them (including how he nearly drowned me on our first date and how I walked into the tent cable at the fair and soaked that poor woman in lemonade). Stuff like that. We were the laughingest table in the restaurant. And the really great thing was I didn't have to worry about being bored or looking like I was staring at Albie or anything like that and ruining the evening, because he and Connor talked about tomorrow's play-off while Genie and I talked about movies and sisters (she has two, too). When he took me home, Connor asked what I'm doing tomorrow while he's running around a dusty field. I said I'm going over to my grandmother's. He said was I planning to forget my phone? I said yes, because last time she took it away from me.

One and a half lies. Nose resting on Madagascar. Guilt squeezing my heart.

SUNDAY

What a day! I suppose I could've gotten sick or something and refused to do the filming, but just to prove how difficult people can be—even your very own self—part of me actually wanted to go. It wasn't like I was doing anything wrong. You know, sneaking off to see another boy. I was sneaking off to spend the day with a carrot. So why should I sit at home letting Zelda beat me at checkers or whatever when I could be doing constructive street theater and having fun? And anyway, I'm getting used to feeling guilty. And I'm getting pretty used to being devious, too. I didn't want the D'Angelos to see me leaving with Louie (and dressed as a head of lettuce) in case they said something to Connor, so I told Louie to pick me up at my gran's because I had to go over to her house first thing. Of course, I didn't want my gran seeing me (dressed as a head of lettuce) leaving with Louie either, because she might say something to my parents. So I put my costume on in that little copse up the road from Gran's, and then I waited for Louie on her corner, standing on the road side of the Langtree Bakery truck so if she looked out her window or went out on her lawn she wouldn't see me. Mr. Langtree saw me, but he didn't recognize me. He wanted to know what I thought I was doing. I said I thought I was waiting for my friend. He said to act like a lettuce and leave. So I started walking in the direction I hoped Louie was coming from. A couple of people came out on their porches to watch me, and the chocolate Lab from the house with the bathtub in the front yard started following me. I was just wishing I'd brought my phone so I could see where Louie was when he pulled up beside me. He leaned out the window and shouted, "Going my way?" Big morning for comedians.

It must be really awful to be a fugitive whose life is nothing but one long lie and complicated deception. If you're hiding from the FBI or the Mafia or something like that. Even if you change your name and move to another town or another country, what good does it do you? Every time there's a knock on the door, your heart must go into toxic shock. Every time you turn a corner or an aisle in the supermarket, you must hold your breath. Just in case. Just in case the person on the other side of the door is a special investigator or a hit man. Just in case the person reading the ingredients on a box of cereal is someone who knows who you really are and is about to start screaming like that woman in *Marathon Man* when she sees the Nazi torturer strolling through Midtown Manhattan looking like a businessman on his lunch hour. Just in case the person at the door or around that corner is your boyfriend. So even though we were MILES from where Connor's game was, I was a wreck for the first couple of hours. My heart did that freezing-like-a-deer-in-headlights thing

every time I saw a red car or a boy wearing a green baseball cap. And I did a lot of jumping into doorways and
behind trucks. (It's pretty epic how popular red cars
and green baseball caps are in Apple Creek.) There must've
been a really big sale on them a while ago. Ely didn't seem
to notice how jiggy I was. But Louie kept giving me looks.
When Ely went to get some water, Louie wanted to know
what was wrong with me. He said I was like a woman on
the verge of a nervous breakdown. I said he was letting
his imagination carry him over the farthest hill and into
a magical land of illusion, as usual. I just wasn't used to
being in the middle of town dressed as a lettuce. Eventually, when none of the cars or caps turned out to be
attached to Connor, I relaxed a little. I wouldn't say I had
as much fun as Mrs. Claws does with a crumpled ball of
paper, but I had patches when I enjoyed myself so much
I forgot about him for minutes at a time. And I relaxed so
much that when Louie asked if he was driving me home
or if I wanted to be dropped off in some stranger's driveway, I said of course I wanted him to drive me home. But
I slouched down in my seat. Louie said, "You know, if you
want, you can ride in the trunk and I'll let you out when
we get there." I said I had no idea what he was talking
about. I was just tired. But I was pretty glad when we
pulled into Lebanon Road. I'd done it! My nose might be

moving into the Middle East, but I'd spent the day with Louie and Ely, and Connor hadn't found out. That bubble of relief lasted for as long as it took me to get out of the car and walk up to the house. Because the second I stepped through the door, Zelda said Grandma wanted me to call her. Right away. I said, "*Grandma*? *Grandma* called *me*?" I had a really bad feeling. Up until then, the president of the United States had called me as many times as my grandmother. And he never sounded urgent. I phoned her right back. Gran said she figured I'd want to know that Connor had called her about half an hour ago wanting to talk to me. You know, because I told him that was where I'd be. OHMYGOD. My life was over. My dreams were ashes blown out to a cold and unforgiving sea. I was going to have to join some cloistered religious order and devote my life to good works to make up for all the hurt I caused. And then my gran said, "I told him you'd just left." I said you did? She said, "I trust you, even if other people don't." If she hadn't been on the other end of a piece of plastic, I would've kissed her. Vicki D'Angelo, World's Number-One Grandmother.

Connor said I gave him my gran's phone number. I said no, I didn't. He said yes, you did. Don't you remember? How could I remember, when I didn't give it to him?

He said yes, you did, Hildy. Did I? Am I really and truly losing my mind? Because if you think about it, I must've given it to him. She's not listed. How else would he get it? And why? I mean, if he wanted her number, he'd ask me. So I am losing my mind. Or is this very early senility creeping in?

If there is a hell, am I going to go there for being a person whose grandmother lies for her? Will I be the sinner there with the longest nose?

MONDAY

Max got back from the world of arts and crafts and mosquito bites on Saturday. Cristina says he looks exactly the same except darker and with a scar where he got hit by an arrow. She was really glad to see him. And vice versa. I said wasn't he worried that you might date somebody else while he was away? She said no. I said and you weren't worried that he might date somebody else while he was away? She said no. I said why not? Cristina said why bother worrying about what might happen? It wouldn't stop it from happening. All it would do is make her unhappy. And then she'd make him unhappy. And then he probably would start looking around. Cristina said and anyway, if Max did cheat on her, *then* there'd be plenty of time to be miserable. And to make him feel really, really bad.

As soon as they got home from work, I went over to give Louie's parents the frame I got them for their anniversary. I had a terrific picture of Louie, Scorsese, and Hitchcock all sitting in Mr. Masiado's chair (Scorsese and Hitchcock are wearing Santa hats and Louie's wearing antlers), so I put that in it. They loved it. Mr. Masiado held it up and said, "Who would've thought when I asked Rose if she wanted to go to the movies she'd someday give birth to Bambi?" Louie and Mrs. Masiado both groaned and rolled their eyes. I asked them what they think the secret of their long and happy marriage is. Mr. Masiado said Mrs. Masiado. Mrs. Masiado said she figured she married the right man. Louie said, "You see? They can't even agree on that!" They were going out for dinner, but Louie'd baked them a cake, and they insisted I have a piece with them. We were all sitting in the living room, digging into our slices, when this face suddenly appeared pressing against the screen door like something out of a horror movie. Mr. Masiado screamed and dropped his plate. It was Connor. He wanted to know if I forgot he was picking me up. I said of course not. Didn't my mom tell him that I wanted to give the Masiados their anniversary present before we went out? He said yes, but not loudly. So I had to take my cake with me. I thought it was going to be one of those Connor-impersonates-a-brick-wall nights, but instead he said he was sorry for scaring Mr. Masiado. He'd forgotten about the anniversary. When my mother said I was across the street, he'd thought I was hanging out with Louie. Connor said, "You know how I get. I can't help it." But he is getting better. He apologized. And he wasn't mad at me. You see? Love will save the day!

TUESDAY

On Saturday, Mr. Donnegal, the Dashers' coach, is having a mighty end-of-summer party for them. Everybody's invited. Including me. All the guys are bringing dates. Connor says he can't wait to show me off. What am I going to wear? I don't have a clue!

It was kind of quiet at the stand today. Ely and I did some juggling and talked. Just about regular stuff. Yakyakyak. He was really funny about some disaster dates he's had. I guess I get a little nervous sometimes when I'm talking to Connor in case I say the wrong thing, so it was nice just to say whatever came into my head. Until some evil spirit rose up from the general pollution and infected my brain, because all of a sudden I heard myself asking Ely if he'd ever been jealous. I couldn't believe I said that. Talk about having a big mouth. Why did I ask him that? He said jealous of what? I said oh, you know. Just in general. He said you mean jealous of people who don't drive fifteen-year-old pickup trucks? Or of people who are under seven feet tall? I said forget it. He said are we talking about Connor? I said of course not. Connor doesn't have a jealous corpuscle in his whole body. He's caring, loving, and protective, but he's definitely not jealous. Ely cocked his head to one side like he wanted to see me from a different angle. He said, "So are we talking about *you*? You go around reading Connor's e-mails and checking his phone messages? I had no idea you counted espionage among your many talents, Hildy." I said yeah. And when I have nothing else to do, I put on a blond wig and a false nose and I go to Café Olé! to see who he's talking to. Ely said I guess he'd recognize you if you went as a lettuce. We couldn't stop laughing. But later I remembered what Ely had said and I wondered if that's what Connor does. Not the blond wig and the nose. The e-mails and messages. Is that how he knew where Gran lives? And then I couldn't believe I'd thought that. Now who's being paranoid? I wonder when I'm going to start becoming a better person.

WEDNESDAY

Connor says not to worry about what I'm wearing to the party. He says I always look good, no matter what. I said you've never seen me with terminal bedhead or when I've had the flu or you wouldn't say that. And I look kind of jaundiced in anything yellow. He said I could wear jeans and waders and my hair could look like it's been electrocuted and I'd still look great to him. (How sweet is that?) Nomi doesn't believe him. She said she once answered the door to Jax when she was hennaing her hair (she thought he was her mother), and he didn't say, "Oh, my darling Nomi, you still look beautiful to me even with what looks like blood dripping down your face and a Gap bag over your head." He screamed.

I've come up with a new theory. I call it the There'll Be Another Train in a Few Seconds Theory of Worry. Because as soon as I stopped worrying about how to convince Gus to lend me that peach silk shirt for the party, I thought of a couple of things I might want to worry about even more. I mean, it is a party. I've never been in a really big group of people with Connor before, but I don't have a good feeling about it. Everybody's going to be shining like sparklers. Laughing. Dancing. Fooling around. Flirting. Even if they're not *really* flirting, they'll look like they are. Connor says it doesn't matter what I wear, but I BEG TO DIFFER. All the girls are going to be dressed up like birthday cakes. Only I can't wear some filmy top or skimpy skirt like everybody else. Connor'll think I'm trying to attract other boys. Especially if he sees anybody actually looking at me. And I can't possibly talk to people. Not in a party kind of way. Especially not boy people. With boys I have to stick to hi. And I can't look at them.

Not for more than a second or two. But the place will be full of boys. How can I not look at them? How can I not talk to them? What am I going to do? Sit next to Connor wearing baggy jeans and a sweatshirt and looking at the floor? I can't spend the night in the bathroom. Can I? Would that even be possible?

THURSDAY

None of my party clothes are going to work. They're either too short, too tight, too thin, or too little. Gus was going shopping, so since Connor was busy, I went with her. I figured that if Connor did see me out with my sister, at least I had a good excuse. She acted like me going with her was the human equivalent of Halley's Comet. Something you only see every seventy-five years if the visibility's good. I said I didn't know what she was making such a major musical production about. It's not like I've never gone shopping with her before. She said this summer it is. She said she's asked me tons of times, and

I always act like she's trying to lure me into the forest to leave me there for wild animals to eat. Maybe I should go shopping with Gus more often. We had a really good time. She's pretty much to fashion what Sherlock Holmes is to crime. She can tell you in half a second whether that top is going to make your neck look too long or whether that color makes you look like you need a blood transfusion. She picked out a couple of things for me that I have to admit were immensely flattering and cool—a sundress, a blouse, and a skirt—but I rejected them all. The dress and the skirt were too short. Gus said, "Too short for what? You're not hiking through the tall grass in them. You're going to a party." Not in one of those. The blouse was too gauzy. "That's why they invented the cami top, Hildy." Right, one step up from a bra. Connor'd love that. But even though I vetoed all her suggestions, we were getting along so well that I asked her if she'd ever gone out with anyone who was jealous. She said, "Jealous?" like it was a word I just made up. I told her about the Countess and how gorgeous she was and what she'd said about her husband never getting jealous. I said I wondered if guys ever got jiggy about Gus because she looks like she does. Gus said just one guy gave her a hard time. Barry Lincoln. She said she ignored it at first because she didn't see him that much and she had a brain-addling crush on him, but then one night they were at a party and he had a nervous breakdown because he found her talking to some other boy. Gus said it was monumental. Barry was yelling and screaming and shoving the other guy. And then he hauled him off to deck him. I said what did you do? Gus dumped a bowl of sour-cream dip over Barry's head and went home. She never spoke to Barry again. He didn't apologize? She said oh, he apologized. But what did that do? If you wipe out an entire village and then say how sorry you are, those people are all still dead.

Went over to Connor's and watched a disaster movie. Disaster movies are cool because if you get involved with kissing, you never really feel like you missed anything.

Connor says there are going to be way over a hundred people at the party on Saturday. That seems a bit excessive. There aren't a hundred people on the team. Not even close. But Coach Donnegal's invited all the local players whether they're Clashers or Timber Wolves or whatever.

FRIDAY

I put orange juice on my cereal this morning. I nearly hit
Green Pickup Guy with a zucchini while Ely and I were
showing him the double-turn cascade this afternoon.
And Ely thinks I packed his sunglasses in with somebody's vegetables. He said he knew I'd bite his head off
for asking, but since he doesn't want any more of his pos-
sessions to end up in someone's soup, were there storm
clouds over paradise or did Zelda whack me in the head
with one of her larger dinosaurs again? I said the sun
was shining on the garden of love and that Zelda's been
remarkably nonviolent lately. Then I told him about the
party. He said he'd never heard of anyone being worried
about going to a party before. What's to worry about? You
go, you eat your weight in snacks, you dance, you argue
with people about what music to play next, and you go
home. I said oh, you know. He said no, he didn't think he
did. I muttered about meeting all these new people and

how stressful it is. He said remember when you were a friendly, outgoing extrovert who enjoyed talking to everyone, no matter how bizarre or difficult they were? Was I?

Today was Connor's last day at work, so he picked me up from the stand. I should never have said anything about him not liking Ely, because even though I still had twenty minutes left of my shift, he wouldn't get out of the car. I noticed Ely didn't bother waving or anything either. Connor just sat there watching us. Like an FBI agent doing surveillance. Only we knew he was there, of course. It made me feel really self-conscious. Ely said I could leave early. He said he felt like he was holding me against my will. Like he was Juliet's father making her finish doing the dishes when poor Romeo was under the balcony waiting for her.

Went over to Connor's. He was putting together a playlist for the party on his iPod. There are a lot of songs the whole team likes. And then there are songs that different players like. And Coach Donnegal has a thing about Bruce Springsteen. Connor said at the last big party he went to, he was dating this girl who spent the whole night making eye contact with some guy from another team. Connor finally got so fed up that he dragged her across the room and shoved her at him. Then he went home. He hasn't been to a party since. But he's really looking forward to this one. Because of me. I feel like the Leader of the Free World. It's a big responsibility. What if I accidentally lead the Free World into a nuclear war?

SATURDAY

Migraine. I went. I saw. I vomited. Will write more if I survive.

SUNDAY

I'm much better today, but last night I thought there were about five hundred very small devils with pitchforks and incredibly sharp hooves inside my head, and they were all trying to stab and kick their way out. I wasn't sick when we first got to the party. I had a little headache, but I figured that was just nerves. Otherwise I was OK. Connor and I held hands. Every time he introduced me to someone, I'd say, *Hi, nice to meet you,* whatever, and then the guy would introduce his date and she'd say, *Hi, nice to meet you,* and then the two of us would smile at each other while the boys talked about baseball or whatever. If Connor introduced me to someone who wasn't with a girl, I'd say, *Hi, nice to meet you,* and then I'd look at Connor while the two of them talked about baseball or whatever. I kept squeezing Connor's hand so he'd glance over and see me looking at him. And then Albie and Genie came over. I guess it was such a relief to have somebody I could talk to without him getting mad at me that I got involved with Genie and forgot to keep looking at Connor, and when I did, he wasn't there. Genie thought he and Albie went for something to eat. She said it's not like they're going to get lost. They'll be back. But I went to look for Connor anyway. Which was harder than you'd think. It was like trying to get through the woods without seeing any trees. People I knew and people I didn't know kept trying to talk to me in a friendly, hey-it's-a-party kind of way. I kept nodding and smiling and pushing past them. I was about a hundred miles out of the town of Nervous and steaming into the city of Panic. Every time someone said something to me, I looked around to see if Connor was watching. *Is this girl an obvious flirt? Is this guy putting the moves on me?* And when some guy actually grabbed my hand and tried to dance, I pulled away so fast he ricocheted off the table behind him. It looked like it was snowing potato chips. I finally found Connor out on the deck, eating a hamburger and talking to Coach Donnegal and some of the other guys on the team. I slipped my arm through his and leaned against him. But by then the devils were already in my head. And the longer I stood there, smiling and looking at Connor, the more enthusiastic they got with hurling their pitchforks around and kick-boxing my eyeballs. It was like a really tiny devils' jamboree. It was Coach Donnegal who noticed I'd turned green. He wanted to know if I was all right. Albie's mother gets migraines, so he's something of an expert. He wanted to know if I was going to throw up. I could only nod. After I was sick, Connor took me home. He was really worried. He kept patting my hand as he drove and telling me I was going to be all right. He went back to the party, but he called my mother five times on the landline to make sure I was OK. That's how worried he was. He said he's never seen anybody actually turn green before. I was almost sorry I missed it.

MONDAY

I stayed in bed yesterday (even Zelda tiptoed around like she was impersonating a mouse, so I must've been sicker than I thought). I slept on and off the whole day. And I had a lot of weird dreams that I don't really remember, but they left me feeling kind of sad. Like I'd lost something but I didn't know what. So even though I felt OK today, I decided to take it really easy. Nomi came over and we sat out on the new really-a-deck-at-last and listened to music and talked. She said she didn't know I got migraines. I said I didn't. Not until Saturday. She said this really is a summer of firsts for you, isn't it? First date. First kiss. First boyfriend. First killer headache from hell. I said don't forget it's also the first time I've dressed as a head of lettuce. Zelda came out and wanted to know what was so funny.

Connor came over tonight. He brought me a get-well present. It's a necklace—a silver heart with our initials engraved on it. He said he was so worried about me yesterday that he went to the jewelry store at the mall during his lunch hour and bought it for me. (How ROMANTIC is that?) We sat out on the really-a-deck, which is much better than sitting on the porch, because there's nobody to see you kissing. Until Gus and Abe Zimmerman showed up. Gus said they had decided to officially open the new deck. Just in time for winter. They had a pack of those Chinese sky lanterns to send off into the night. You're supposed to make a wish. So of course everybody came out to light a lantern and make a wish. My mom was afraid we were going to start a fire, but even Zelda got her lantern in the air without torching Lebanon Road. When we were finally alone again, Connor wanted to know what my wish was. I said you can't tell your wish, or it won't come true. He said he bet it was the same thing he wished. Since anyone who isn't me who so much as glances at this diary will immediately be struck down by a bolt of lightning, I can say here that I doubt that. I wished I'd never have a migraine again. Ever. But I didn't say that to Connor. I didn't want to ruin the love mood. I said that wasn't much of a bet. And then we melted into each other's arms. Bliss.

TUESDAY

Connor wanted to know what I'm going to do while he's away. What I'm doing starting Friday is staying with Nomi, because there's a big Labor Day old junk convention and her parents are leaving her alone again, and on Sunday the other girls are coming over for a pajama party. Not that I told Connor any of that. I said, "Not much." I said we're having the inaugural barbecue on the new deck on Labor Day, but otherwise I'll just be hanging around the house. Psyching myself up for going back to school. Missing him. Hoping he doesn't fall in the river or get stabbed with a hook. Sending him texts and e-mails he won't get until he gets back to civilization.

I told Connor what the Countess said about dancing on the silver clouds of love. He thought it was great. So he declared tonight Dancing on the Silver Clouds of Love

Night. Otherwise known as sitting on the deck watching YouTube videos. We were having such a good time that I forgot to be careful and said he had to see the one Louie and I did of Hitchcock and Scorsese arguing over who was going to sit in Mr. Masiado's chair. Connor checked the time. He said he had a lot to do tomorrow and he better get going. I felt like a little kid whose balloon suddenly popped.

Is it possible that love means always feeling like you've done something wrong?

WEDNESDAY

Our LAST NIGHT TOGETHER of the summer. We went to his secret beach. Connor brought a picnic. He even brought candles! We wrote I LOVE YOU in the sand surrounded by a big heart. He'd put some of our favorite songs on his iPod, and we sat listening to them while we watched the sun go down. The candles kept blowing out. And it started to rain. But we still had a great time.

Lovelovelove . . .

THURSDAY

Ely wanted to know what was wrong with me today. I said, "Nothing." And there wasn't. I was in a really good mood. If I was corn, I'd be popping. He said that was what he meant. I wasn't jumpy. Or moody. Or quiet. Or preoccupied. Or acting like we'd never been introduced. I said probably I was in such a good mood because after this week, I'll only see him on Saturdays. That would put anybody's spirits over the satellite dish. He threw a patty-pan squash at me, but I caught it and threw it back. Next thing you know, we were walking around the table doing cascades and fountains. A couple of cars stopped to watch. Later Broccoli Man came by. But he left the car door open, and while he was trying to pick out exactly one pound of carrots, Monsanto the killer cat got in. Broccoli Man didn't notice till he got in himself and started to pull out. I don't know which of them screamed louder. He drove into the fence. Ely and I couldn't stop laughing.

Went over to Louie's tonight. He said to what do I owe this honor? If I'd thought about what to say before saying it, I would've said I'd decided to take pity on him. But I didn't. I said I missed him. Which is true. When my head wasn't hurting so much and I could actually think again, I'd been thinking about Louie a lot while I was recovering from the migraine. He said it's not like he moved or anything. I said yeah, well, you know. He said yeah, he did know. He said he missed me, too.

FRIDAY

It's been all systems go since I got to Nomi's. I had to come over at the crack of dawn for the big briefing because, since her parents aren't back till Monday night,

Mr. Slevka wanted to make really sure we knew what to do if there was a tornado or a wolf attack or something like that. He made a list of things we MUST DO before we leave the house or go to bed, and we're supposed to check everything off on it each time. The good news is that he had an expert come and look at the alarm, so at least we don't have to worry about Mr. Janofski making any sudden marine landings in the living room. Meanwhile, back in the kitchen, Mrs. S taped a sheet of emergency numbers on the door of the refrigerator. She said it's the one place we're guaranteed to see it. She has every number on it except the Pentagon's. I swear. She even has my parents' number on it. I said I'm not ET; I can manage to call home, Mrs. Slevka. She said that's what you say now. We slouched around most of the morning, but then we went into town for lunch. It took us an hour and a half to leave the house because of Mr. Slevka's checklist. Nomi figures it's easier to get out of a high-security prison. We were going to the diner, but Cristina and Max were in the Bear Café, so we went in there. Max had us falling off our chairs with his stories of camp life. I never knew how funny poison ivy can be! After lunch me and Nomi wandered around town. Ran into some kids from school who were wandering around too. Hung out with them for a while comparing rumors. (Did Ms. Veber really marry a forest ranger and leave Redbank? Did Mr. Donough become a monk? Are they going to make us wear uniforms?) Then we stopped by Maggie's. Sara was there. She'd had a fight with Kruger, so she was hiding out at the Pryces'. The four of us ended up playing a hysterical game of Pictionary. Mrs. Pryce felt sorry for me and Nomi having to microwave our own meal, so she asked us to stay for supper. There was no sign of Mr. Pryce or the barbecue, so we figured it was safe. It was late by the time we got back to Casa Slevka. It wasn't until I was brushing my teeth that I realized I don't have my phone! It seems impossible, but it's true. I was in such a hurry this morning that I left it charging in my room. I haven't thought of it all day. Or of Connor! How amazing is that?

SATURDAY

It was really hot and muggy, so we went to the mall with Cristina and Sara. Got things for school. Then Nomi and I picked up some stuff for tomorrow and went over to Casa D'Angelo for supper. My mom had made lasagna. You don't want to miss my mom's lasagna even if you're living the dream with Nomi. And I wanted to pick up my phone. Of course. I'd promised Connor I'd text him even if he couldn't get the texts till he was on his way back. Wound up playing cards for hours with the whole family. Including Gus and Abe. But my phone's disappeared! How is that possible? I know exactly where I left it. It was right there, attached to the charger. Zelda swears she didn't touch it. I said so who did? One of your dinosaurs? She wanted to know why she gets blamed for everything. Nobody else touched it either. (Of course.) Mom thinks I must've taken it off the charger and put it somewhere when I was rushing around so much. I said I don't remember that. She said well, that's the point. I said well, I guess it's either that or the ghost. My dad drove us back to Nomi's.

3 A.M.

Major thunderstorm, but that's not what woke us. What woke us was the alarm. Nomi thinks somebody was trying to get in. You know, because Mr. Slevka had the expert come, and she said it's working the way it's supposed to. I said experts are wrong all the time. They're so wrong it's amazing anybody ever listens to them. And even if the expert was right, I figure the storm could've set it off. I mean, it's all electricity, isn't it? But Nomi said she heard things. I said of course you hear things. It's an old house, and everything's rattling because of the wind and the rain. You can't walk across the bathroom without hearing the floorboards creak ten minutes later. She said she didn't mean the rattling or the creaking. She meant an intruder. She wouldn't stop till we had checked every window and door twice. Then she wanted to look in every closet and cupboard. I said it's not like somebody's going to hide behind the canned vegetables, Nomi. She said why not? Maybe it's a trained robber monkey. Did I think of that? The weird thing is that by the time we'd checked out anything with hinges that opens (including the piano), I was as wound up as Nomi. A branch or something bounced off the window, and I nearly went into cardiac arrest. I said it's just like jealousy, isn't it? Nomi wanted to know what was just like jealousy. I said thinking there's an intruder. The more you think about it, the more you convince yourself. It keeps building like a snowball till if you see a coin on the floor, you think the burglar dropped it. Nomi asked how I knew that was just like being jealous. I said it's called using your imagination. They are both about being paranoid. It's not that big a leap. Nomi said, "Are we talking about Connor Bowden

here?" I said that it's not really jealousy with Connor. She said making you take pictures of yourself in closets? Checking up that you're really where you said you'd be? That's not jealousy? I said no. It may look like that, but it isn't. She said what is it? I said love. But sometimes he gets a little carried away. Nomi said, "You're wrong, Hildy. It isn't love; it's jealousy."

SUNDAY

Everybody else has finally crashed, but I can't sleep. It's been the most incredible night. So incredible that I don't even know where to start. So I guess I'll start with Maggie, Cristina, and Sara coming over. That was just before it began storming again. We decided to sleep in the family room in the basement, because it was way hot and humid again today and it's cooler down there. Plus there's enough room for all the sleeping bags and for us to spread out. And there's a bathroom and a mini fridge. So we don't have to keep going upstairs or

downstairs for stuff. We listened to music and played Ping-Pong. Then we played cards. Then we ordered pizza. After that, we were ready to hunker down and watch a couple of movies. Maggie was doing Nomi's nails. Cristina was crimping Sara's hair. Typical slumber party. We were having so much fun that none of us could understand why it was the first time we'd done it all summer. (And now it was the last time we'd do it all summer.) Anyway, we were on our first intermission when Nomi thought she heard something. I said oh, no, not again. She told me to shush. She turned down the music. We couldn't hear anything but the storm, really. At least Maggie, Cristina, Sara, and I couldn't hear anything. Cristina said anyway, old houses creak more than rusty swings. Nomi said it didn't sound like her old house creaking; it sounded like someone trying to get in. Sara said so let them try. You have the alarm. Nomi and I looked at each other. It was one of those uh-oh looks. We hadn't put the alarm on yet. The pizza man came and we ate. And then we were talking and recovering from pizza bloat. And then we started the DVD. So we hadn't done the whole routine with the checklist and everything. You know, because it takes hours, and we wanted to hang out, not lock up Fort Knox. We were going to do that later. I said maybe we should put it on now. Then it'll be done.

Nomi said what if there's already somebody up there? I didn't think there was. I said it's not like we left the front door wide open. We locked it. We just didn't put the alarm on. And everything else was locked. Nomi said was it? After we opened the living-room windows to get a breeze, did we lock them again? I couldn't remember. But probably we did. It's the kind of thing you do automatically. Turn off the stove. Turn off the iron. Lock the windows. I said you're winding yourself up again. There isn't anybody up there. I was sure of it. And then we heard what could definitely be somebody shutting the window they'd opened that we didn't lock. Nomi turned the music off completely. Sara whispered that they were going up the stairs. Cris whispered that she didn't hear anything. Maggie poked her to be quiet. That time, I did hear something that could've been someone — or some-ones — crossing the living room. The only light we'd left on was in the kitchen, so they were going really slowly. And then we all heard someone trip over that extra step when you reach the hall. We didn't know what to do. Go up after them? Flee? Maggie said we should lock the basement door and call the police. But the basement door doesn't lock since the time Mrs. Slevka got trapped when she was doing the laundry. So Nomi called the police. We couldn't hear their side of the conversation, but Nomi kept saying, "Well, no . . . Well, no, we—" and sighing and rolling her eyes, so we figured they weren't going to send sixteen squad cars with their sirens shrieking anytime soon. I said we should go up and set off the alarm, because that would freak them out and bring Mr. Janofski running. Everybody thought that was a great idea. Sara thought we should have weapons. Some blunt, heavy objects. But Nomi said we wanted to surprise and disable whoever it was, not actually kill them. She dashed into the utility room and came back with a clutch of spray cans. Starch. Air freshener. Cleaners. Armed, we tiptoed up the stairs. Only when we got to the door that leads into the kitchen, we could hear footsteps coming back downstairs. I guess because I've been lying so much that I'm used to thinking quickly when adrenaline is galloping through my bloodstream, I felt strangely calm. I told Nomi to go out the back and get Mr. Janofski and his bare hands. The rest of us crept back to the basement. What were the chances they'd come down there? If they were smart, they were going to go through the living room and the study and grab cameras and laptops and stuff like that. And then they'd run. But just in case for some bizarre reason they figured the Slevkas kept their valuables in the cellar, we lined up on either side of the stairs, cans at the ready. It seemed like hours passed while we waited to be rescued by either the marine or the police. And then the door to the basement opened. We all stopped breathing. A lone figure stood on the top step for a minute or two. We couldn't actually see him, but we could feel him. We had a light on, so I guess he was listening for voices. I signaled to Sara and Maggie that we'd jump him on the count of three. He started down. I held up one finger. He reached the middle. Two. He stepped into the basement. Three! We jumped out, spraying and screaming. Nomi and Mr. Janofski must've been pretty close behind him, because when he tried to run back up the stairs, he ran straight into Mr. Janofski in his pajamas and robe. Mr. Janofski said, "Well, what do we have here?" And all of us answered at once, "It's Connor!" As far as I can remember, we all sounded surprised.

I have to crash now. More tomorrow. When maybe it'll all make more sense.

MONDAY

It doesn't. Make more sense. Nomi, Maggie, Cristina, Sara, and I all agree on that. When we woke up, we all looked at each other and Sara said, "We didn't have some communal nightmare, did we? It did really happen." Nomi said as bright, creative, and imaginative as we all are, we couldn't have made up last night. And *who* could?

So back to what happened. The police arrived while I was still explaining to Mr. Janofski that what we had there was my boyfriend, not an unknown intruder. Mr. Janofski wasn't too impressed. He didn't let go of Connor. He said, "*This* is your boyfriend? Your boyfriend broke into your friend's house?" He said it more than once. Then the police showed up. They were a lot less interested than Mr. Janofski. They thought it was just teenagers fooling around, and they gave us all a warning about wasting their time and left. But there was no way Mr. Janofski was going to keep his mouth shut, and we knew it. We knew it because he said, "I'll have to tell your parents, Nomi. You know that, don't you?" Nomi said, "Oh, don't worry, Mr. Janofski. I'll tell them myself." She was glaring at Connor. I wondered if she'd always disliked him so much. After Mr. Janofski marched back across the lawn, Nomi, Maggie, Cristina, and Sara all went inside while Connor explained to me less vaguely than he had in front of the others what he was doing climbing in through the Slevkas' window when he was supposed to be camping by a river. What happened was that the Bowden men came back early from their fishing trip because Connor's granddad's gout started acting up. Connor called me on the landline while he and his dad were driving back, but of course I wasn't there. Zelda answered. I figure he was already a little charged up because he expected to find all these messages from me when he could get a signal again and there weren't any. Zelda told him I was at a party at Nomi's. If she said "pajama party," he didn't hear that part. But he definitely heard the "Nomi" and the "party" parts. He knew it! He'd been right all along. Women can't be trusted. I told him I'd be sitting at home missing him, but the minute he turned his back, I was partying with my friends. So he came right over. He wanted to catch me in the act. Not the act where I was dancing and eating pretzels without him. The act where I was with another guy. It didn't discourage him for even a blink when he got to the Slevkas' and there weren't any signs of a party. He figured we were all making out in the dark. That's why he broke in like that. I asked him if he realized how much he'd scared us. For all we knew, he was armed and dangerous. We were terrified. He said he didn't mean to scare us. How could he? He didn't think we were there all by ourselves watching a movie. He thought we were having a party. With lots of boys. I said and did he realize how much he'd embarrassed me? Having your boyfriend break into your best friend's house makes him look crazy and you look like a fool. He said he didn't mean to embarrass me either. It was just that he was really worried. I said that if a person was so worried, he would knock on the door. He said not necessarily. I said and anyway, he *did* mean to embarrass me. He thought he was going to make a big scene and humiliate me in front of EVERYBODY. Connor said, "Well, I was mad." I said he wasn't the only one. And I marched back into the house and slammed the door. Set off the alarm, and it wasn't even on.

Nomi said I should never have given Connor her address. I said I didn't. She said, "Oh. You think Zelda did?" I said Zelda's lucky to know her own address, never mind somebody else's.

274

My phone was exactly where I'd left it when I got home this morning. Nobody knows anything about where it was or how it managed to put itself back in my room and plug itself in. I believe that Zelda and my dad had nothing to do with it. Zelda would've destroyed it somehow if she'd taken it. And my dad wouldn't interfere like that unless I was a car. That leaves my mom and Gus. They're like Batman and Robin when it comes to interfering (only without the masks and the Batmobile). Which, considering how Connor acted, may not be such a bad thing.

So it was the big inaugural barbecue today. Everybody came. Gran said she heard what happened with Connor. I pretended to be shocked and astounded by this. She said she was glad to see I was taking it with my usual good humor. She said it sounded like we girls had been very brave and level-headed. That was just what Mr. Janofski said. He said we should all consider joining the Marines. Gran said you know it's not healthy for either of you, when someone's so possessive and controlling. I had to ask. I said, "Is that why you lied for me when I told him I was with you and I wasn't?" Gran said yes. She said love is about trust, not fear. (My mom and Gus aren't the only caped crusaders in the family.) Then she wanted to know what I'm going to do. I said you mean am I going to join the Marines? She said no, Hildegard. About Connor. I said I didn't know. Which is true. One minute I never want to speak to him again, and the next I'm remembering some sweet thing he did or funny thing he said and feeling bad. Should I follow my heart or my head? Sometimes I think heart, because the heart's about feelings. Other times I think head, because it's my feelings that got me into this mess. Gran said maybe I could follow both of them.

Needless to say, Gran wasn't the only person who'd heard what happened. You can't pull a stunt like that and think Nomi, Maggie, Sara, and Cristina won't tell everybody they ever met. I could tell all the guys knew, because they were all super nice to me and goofing around, trying to make me laugh. But only Ely and Louie came out and said anything. Ely said he's still available if I want to talk. His office is open any hour of the day or night, and his services include juggling lessons and stupid jokes. I said thanks. Louie gave me a DVD he'd put together to cheer me up. He said, "Don't worry, Hildy. My offer to marry you if we're still single when we hit forty is still on the table." I said that made me feel a lot better.

*　　*　　*

Connor's called and texted me sixteen times today. He wants us to talk, but I told him I need a few days' chill time before I see him again. You don't go on a diet and then walk straight into a bakery. Connor's really, really sorry. Really. Nomi says he should be. Connor says he knows what he did was really stupid (let's not leave out illegal, too), but he only did it because he loves me so much. Does he? Is that what love means to Connor? Not the breaking and entering; the not trusting me to even cross the street without trying to betray him. If you follow that logic, the next thing is to lock me up in a cage. Nomi's wrong—electronic tagging wouldn't be good enough. He'd know where I am, but he wouldn't know what I'm doing. Or with who. It would make him go nuts.

Was feeling a little like you do after Christmas. All that build-up and excitement and running around, and then you're left with a pile of dead pine needles on the floor and a bag full of used wrapping paper. Couldn't stop thinking about Connor. So I watched Louie's DVD. It's all clips of videos he made of the Mob over the last few years. The Christmas we all went to chop down our own trees. (And discovered that if the settling of America had depended on us, we'd still be living on ships in the harbor.) The Halloween party where everyone came as their favorite movie character and Scorsese came as the lion in *The Wiz-ard of Oz*. (He ate his mane.) The time we went tubing. The time Ely's pickup set itself on fire. Nomi trying to carry her hundred-pound pumpkin. Grady asleep on the porch. Ely and me dressed as vegetables. All stuff like that. It definitely cheered me up.

TUESDAY

I'm actually happy to be back at school. I think because it's so normal. I almost feel like I've been in some bizarre country all summer, eating crickets and riding around on wildebeests, where I didn't really get the rules. And now I'm back in the land of pizza and automobiles and I know what to expect. So even though it's boring and about as exotic as cornflakes, it's kind of a relief.

Connor's still texting. He says I owe it to him to give him another chance. So he did something stupid. Everybody makes mistakes. And of course that's totally true. People do stupid things all the time. I'm surrounded by people who are always doing stupid things. I do stupid things. But what Connor did wasn't in the same league as setting fire to something when you barbecue. Or dressing up like a carrot. Or backing into the mailbox. Or even putting all your dinosaurs in the washing machine. What Connor did was wrong. The really weird thing is I don't feel that mad at him anymore. Not *that* mad. I kind of feel more tired than angry. I told him I'll meet him on Friday after school.

It's not just the breaking and entering that was wrong. How can you love somebody if you can't trust him? How can he love you if he doesn't trust *you*?

Nomi says "love" is obviously one of those words that means different things to different people. Like "fun." Or "important." Maybe boys shouldn't come with a manual. Maybe they should come with a dictionary.

Ten texts, five e-mails, and a message on my Facebook page saying *Please, please, please* from Connor. I'm not answering, but not because I'm not tempted. I keep imagining him saying *Please, please, please* and the look on his face when I say I forgive him. That smile. Like just seeing me makes him happy. Only then I see that other look on his face. The one when he's mad at me for nothing. And it's like just seeing him makes me unhappy.

WEDNESDAY

Part of me just wants to forget it all and go back to the way things were with Connor. Or at least the way I thought they were. But then I start thinking about the way things really were. Thinking's like potato chips. The more you do of it, the more you want to do. When you open a bag of chips and you swear you're only going to have a handful and instead you eat the whole thing. I can't seem to stop. Thinking, not eating potato chips. So now even the things I thought were OK or pretty normal are starting to look not OK and nowhere near normal. Like the way Connor always checked to see if I was where I said I'd be. How he just popped up at pottery and yoga and Gran's like that. People disappearing on me from Facebook. Connor having a pretty good working knowledge of my addresses and phone numbers. (He must've spent practically as much time on my phone and in my e-mail account as I do.) And getting all warped if I saw my friends. I thought I understood about him being jiggy and everything, but now I'm not sure I do. He's the only person I know who acts like that. (Well, him and Barry Lincoln, I guess.) I'm not saying there aren't other people like that, just that I don't know them. The Mob guys might get upset if you finished all the cookies, but not if you said hello to a kid in your art class. It's embarrassing, Connor not wanting me to see my friends. Especially since I'm pretty sure they all knew. Comments have been made. And if they didn't know before the break-in, they sure as sunset know now. I can't decide which of us is the biggest dope. Connor or me. Do I really want to go back to that?

But it wasn't all sulks and silence and me walking into things. What about all the good times we had? All the fun? We had a lot of fun. We had really good times. When I wasn't bouncing up and down on the rusty trampoline of love, I was definitely dancing on its silver clouds. That's my problem. I can't forget all that. So one minute I feel like if I'd caught him coming in the Slevkas' window, I would've slammed it down on his fingers. The next minute all I can think of is when we fell in the lake. And our picnics at the secret beach. And how he carried me on his back when I hurt my ankle. And all the sweet or funny things he said and did. Maybe love doesn't make you a better person. Maybe it does just make you nuts.

THURSDAY

Connor sent me a text every hour today. *I love you.* Every hour. I do believe he thinks he loves me, but like Nomi said, you don't really know what he means by that. I don't remember anybody ever defining love as a burning desire to hunt down the other person like you're an FBI agent and they're a terrorist. And in all the really romantic scenes I can think of, the guy never says to the girl that now that they're in love, she can't go shopping with her friends or walk down the street with her eyes open anymore. He never puts his arms around her and says, "Darling, now that you're mine, you can't hang out with anybody else ever again. No, not even to go bowling."

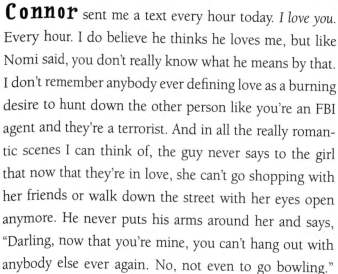

Also, I don't think I've ever heard of love giving you migraines.

Good-night text from Connor. He was watching for falling stars. He said remember all the times we sat out watching them together? And what about all our plans? He misses me and he can't wait to see me tomorrow. I texted back *I miss you too*. But I forced myself not to look for any stars dropping out of the sky. I thought I loved him. Do I? If I do love him, does that mean I'm not allowed to like anybody else?

FRIDAY

We met in Shep's Diner. At the back booth. Connor looked great. (Much better than the last time I saw him. Spray starch isn't really a good look. Not even for someone as cute as he is.) My heart did a double cascade when I saw him. I was so happy that I forgot about being cool for a minute and ran up and kissed him. He kissed me back. I'd almost forgotten how good he smells. I felt like I could've stayed in that hug forever. But we were blocking the aisle, so we had to sit down. Connor tried to pull me into the seat beside him, but I reminded him that we were supposed to be talking. Seriously. Not pretending nothing had happened. So he sat on one side and I sat on the other. He asked how I was and I asked how he was. How school was. All that kind of thing. Then we got down to business. He said again how sorry he is about what happened and how much he's missed me and how he doesn't know why he acted like such an idiot. He just can't seem to help himself. He loves me so much. Sitting there with our feet kind of touching under the table and everything, it was just the way it used to be. I kept thinking that it wasn't as if we hadn't had fights before. And we'd always patched things up. Hadn't we? Like people do. Only there was a difference this time. This time I didn't feel guilty. Not even a tiny bit. This time I felt that I was completely in the right. I didn't have any excuses for Connor left. Only Connor didn't know that. He thought it really was the way it used to be. So after he'd said how sorry he was some more and we'd laughed about Mr. Janofski in his pajamas, I must've said I forgave him. Because then he said that none of this would've happened if I'd told him the truth about where I was going to be in the first place. He'd been rubbing his foot against mine. I pulled mine away. I said are you saying it was all my fault? Connor said what he was saying was that it wasn't all his fault. I said I'm not the one who broke into somebody's house, you know. He said but he wouldn't have done that if I'd stayed at home like I said I was going to do. Instead of lying. What's he supposed to do if I lie to him? I can't really get mad at him for being upset about that. Only it looked like I could. I might have said I forgave him, but I could tell that I was still mad. More than *still* mad. Now I was mad for all the times that I didn't get mad, too. All the times he wouldn't talk to me or was angry over nothing and wouldn't even tell me what it was. All the times he made me feel like I was a horrible person. It wasn't just the Slevkas' he broke into. He broke into my heart. I felt like somebody finally turned the lights on. So at last I could see that I wasn't where I thought I was at all. I thought I was in some kind of paradise, but really I was in this tiny, dark cell. I didn't yell or anything, though. Actually, I felt really calm. I said what difference does it make, Connor? I wasn't doing anything wrong. I was hanging out with my friends. What'd you think I was going to do all weekend? Sit in my room? He said yes. That's what I'd said, and that's what he thought I was going to do. Like that was perfectly reasonable. I said but if you didn't get all wound up every time I wanted to hang out with my friends, I would've told you. He said exactly. I didn't tell him because if I did, he would've been upset, and then I would've stayed home like I should have. I know that puppets aren't real, so this could never happen, but I felt like I was a puppet who suddenly looked up and noticed the strings and this dude standing over her making them move. And I knew exactly what I had to do. I said, "You know what, Connor? I've finally figured out what the difference between a car and a relationship is. Besides the seats and the engine and everything." I stood up. I think he thought I was going to come around and sit with him, because he moved over a little. And he kind of smiled like he thought I was teasing him. "OK, I give up, Hildy. What's the difference between a car and a relationship?" So I told him. Only a car has a passenger. He wanted to know what that meant. I said it meant that in a relationship, both of you are responsible for driving. So even though he acted like a jerk and pushed me around, I didn't stop him. But I was stopping him now. "We're done," I said. "I'm going home. And if you're interested, I'm spending the night with my friends." I took the phone he bought me out of my bag and put it on the table. Don't call me, 'cause I won't call you.

SATURDAY

Stayed over at Nomi's last night. We made chocolate cupcakes and talked till we couldn't keep our eyes open anymore. I said I figured I'd learned more about love from Connor in a couple of months than I'd learned from the whole world in seventeen years. But I think I was right that love's about everything not being me, me, me. It has to be a partnership. The problem with Connor was that it was all about him. What *he* wanted. How *he* felt. Never about me and what I wanted or how I felt. Nomi said, "Excuse me, Hildegard, but isn't that what I said? That somebody was confusing love with a fascist dictatorship?" Nomi said that maybe in the future I should make all prospective boyfriends take a test before I go out with them. The Hidden Shallows and Murky Depths Test. I said you can't ask someone if he's insanely jealous and going to walk off a pier if he thinks you're looking at some fisherman. She said no, but you could ask if he has a secret desire to wear a military uniform and have people salute him. How hilarious is that? There were a couple of hours after I left Connor in the diner when I thought I might never laugh again. At least not for a really long time. But even though I know I'm going to feel sad for a while, the laughing's definitely not going to be a problem.